THE MOUSETRAP MURDERS

Abraham Lopez

This is a work of fiction. Names, characters, businesses, places, events, locales, and incidents are either the products of the author's imagination or used in a fictitious manner. Any resemblance to actual persons, living or dead, or actual events is purely coincidental.

Copyright © 2023 Abraham Lopez

All rights reserved.

ISBN: 9798393274016

For Jon
May I see you around a Snow Mesa campfire again, Dad

The Mousetrap Manifesto - Prologue

THE MOUSETRAP MURDERS us all.

It is voracious, never sated. It consumes all who enter and leaves no trace of dignity or integrity.

It murders most in their sleep but some in broad daylight.

It is remorseless.

The masses barely realize the walled maze around them, much less that they are but rodents scurrying for a morsel at the center—a center which, often, does not exist.

So it is time.

Time to wake up my compatriots, wherever I may encounter them. Wake them up and force them to smell what two centuries of the racism, intolerance, and hate spewing from the festering wound of White oppression truly reeks of.

For only those of us with eyes truly open, minds truly tuned to this oppression, can be ready; can possibly know what must be done:

Razing and reconstructing a country in our own image.

But to begin, the scales of Justice must be tipped away from those oppressors. And for that, two things are necessary: leverage and a fulcrum.

And I shall supply both.

I realize that this message, my manifesto, may only be realized once I am gone. But so be it. For it is foundational for all the disenfranchised citizens of this nation, this supposed "United" country that is balanced upon a crumbling lie that deems everyone equal under its Constitution.

This message is also for all those who are not yet awakened but need a good kick in the ass to join the new Revolution.

But mine—ours—will be a true Revolution that recognizes the importance not only of Equality but of Equity. It will expose the lies that men like Jefferson, Adams, and Washington deceived the people with for centuries.

No, their fable was but a shadow of Equality. Under that shadow, they and their treacherous ilk pulled the levers of power. Their White Brotherhood denied the Other: minorities, women—even their own women—a taste of true freedom. We would only taste the bitterness of an ersatz freedom that could be pulled from us at a moment's notice.

This was according to their design.

Their mousetrap.

It is this Mousetrap that I intend to dismantle. Forever.

> *"A king must be unafraid of burning jesters in order to keep his kingdom. Kings who lower themselves to the level of these vermin become food for vermin soon enough. Great men must know their greatness, must accept it wholly if they are to attain the shield of providence. Woe to those imbued with this glorious gift who continue to scurry in doubt along the narrow walls of mediocrity's labyrinth. God spits upon such men."*

Truly great men must understand their greatness to make the changes they were born to make.

They do this to break the Mousetrap. That machine responds to the lever pulls of an operator. It can allow men and women to be free or enclose them in despair. In the right hands it exacts retribution from those who have ill-used it for far too long.

These Great Men, these given few, must also understand the SACRIFICES they must make.

Sometimes those sacrifices must be of Pride.
Sometimes of Time.
And sometimes the sacrifice must be Human.
I am just such a Great Man.
And I am prepared to make those sacrifices.
Yours truly,
The Fulcrum

Part I: Run Of Bad Luck

Regrets are flowers grown in bitter soil,
Watered with abundant strife,
Brittle petals swirl upon the memory of toil,
Becoming ashes of a former life.
-The Death Row Inmate

_NE

IN TWENTY-FOUR hours, Julian Gutierrez would be a jailed man.

When he woke up, he sensed the musty cocoon of his car sheltering him from the fall air. The sweaty wetness sticking his clothes to his body seeped through Julian's mental fog. His forehead throbbed against the steering wheel.

As Julian's haze lifted, his eyes focused on the instrument panel. The stiffness in his neck and lower back meant he had been in that position for some time. He straightened to find every window fogged.

Why am I here?

Fighting the overwhelming desire to slip back into unconsciousness, the alien thought struck him that he should open the driver's side door. Julian fumbled for the handle in the dark with all the grace of a newborn foal. His fingers brushed cold, flat metal. With an effort, he pulled the lever until a distinct and somehow satisfying *click* sounded, followed by plaintive dinging as the door opened.

A rush of cool but humid air raised gooseflesh on his exposed arms and legs. The dam of his mental haze burst, loosing a torrent of pent-up thoughts.

I was running, wasn't I? Sure I was, the 10K is next week, so I was running the outer loop. Or wait, was that yesterday? Didn't I run by that old church, the one with the screwed-up bell tower? Shit, what time is it? How ...

Julian staggered out of the car and fell flat on his ass next to the back bumper. The wooded Virginia landscape swam in front of him, making him nauseous. He closed his eyes and held his head until the feeling passed. Then he gathered himself, got up, and drew in a full breath to clear his head.

The day's events filtered back to him. He'd parked near the baseball field as usual to get in his daily five-mile run. His route followed a paved trail at the edge of town near the Spotsylvania Civil War memorial battlefield. He'd changed into his running shorts and t-shirt in a nearby public restroom and begun running as the sun set.

The late October afternoon had been chilly, but he should have been finished and back to his car with just a bit of sunlight left.

But Julian couldn't remember how or when he'd gotten back to his car. He looked down at his Nike GPS watch, a gift from his sister. It was dead, its battery spent. So he peeked back into the car. The digital dashboard clock read 11:03.

Over five hours. How is that possible?

Julian cast anxious looks all around, sure someone was watching him. He scrabbled for his keys, wanting only to get the hell out of there.

The keys weren't tied on the top knot of his shoelace as usual. Or in his running shorts' pockets. His nausea returned, along with panic, when a final puzzle piece fell into place.

He'd pushed the noise into the background, but the car's chime had been going off since he'd opened the door. Because the keys were in the ignition.

Julian was certain *he* hadn't put them there, but there they were nonetheless. He jumped back in the driver's seat, slammed the door shut, and started the car. The windows were still somewhat fogged, so he lowered the side windows as he sped away, all the while struggling to put his seat belt on.

He had gone two blocks before he realized he hadn't turned his headlights on.

Lucky I wasn't pulled over.

T_O

JULIAN STAGGERED INTO his second-story apartment at just past 11:30. He opened the refrigerator and drank almost a liter of chilled water in three deep gulps, the last of which gave him a pang of side stitch.

He stood there, the refrigerator light casting his hazy shadow across the kitchen floor of his one-bedroom apartment.

Julian's memory was still murky. *This must be what it's like to be on drugs, or blackout drunk.*

A shy, reserved guy; the type people called "nice," Julian didn't get into trouble. At least he hadn't since his teenage years. But intuition told him he was in trouble now. He couldn't explain it, but he felt the walls of his apartment closing in.

On instinct, Julian turned on every light to beat back the shadows. He undressed, taking his watch off and putting it on the USB charger next to his computer. Then he turned on the shower and stared at himself in the bathroom mirror as the water heated up.

The figure looking back seemed a stranger, with bloodshot eyes and a haggard expression of fright. Fog formed at the mirror's edges and encroached on his face, trapping him in a two-dimensional world. He looked away and plunged himself into the scalding cascade of water.

Julian emerged, red and aching, but with a refreshing clarity of thought. Free of the haze that had followed him since he'd awoken, he walked into the living room while drying himself with a terrycloth towel. He was still dabbing his wet hair when he glanced at his laptop and froze.

The screen showed a map. In one regard it was familiar. The Nike watch had powered up and downloaded his run information: pace, elevation change, and route.

Along with *Total Distance: 8.14 miles.*

That last number had Julian mystified. And worried.

As he was training for the 10K race he'd signed up for, he'd planned to take an easy pace on a path he'd run several times.

But he didn't know the path displayed on his laptop—at least not most of it. The first portion circled through the forest back to where he'd parked his car, as planned. But two miles in, his path had veered at a right angle *into* the woods.

He tried to remember anything at all before he woke up in his car. Did he remember his run? Had he maybe fallen, hit his head, and wandered back to his car?

If so, he had traipsed around the forest for an extra three miles, and at a snail's pace, too.

Average Pace: 24:22/mile

He threw on some sweatpants and a tank top, then sat down to examine the run information further. According to the displayed elevation changes, the path he'd taken went over rough terrain. He'd meandered for a couple more miles, then stopped in the middle of the forest for some time before heading back to the paved path to his car.

What the hell's going on? Did I have a stroke or something? Julian racked his brain for a reasonable answer to what he saw on the screen. He reflexively probed his head for bruising but felt no tenderness.

Another thought occurred to him: *What if my watch is wrong?* What if he did fall and bang the timepiece against a tree or the concrete? Would that even affect a GPS watch? He didn't think so, but he grasped for any answer that didn't imply he was losing his mind.

The stray image of a muddy smudge flashed in Julian's

head. *Where did I see that?*

He closed his eyes. Soon he was drifting into a shallow, uneasy doze. Then it came to him.

After his anxious drive home, he'd parked his car outside his apartment complex and stepped onto the sidewalk. The streetlight had illuminated him as he'd walked under it. He'd been about to go up the flight of stairs to his apartment when he'd realized he hadn't locked the car door. Turning around to do so and listening for the polite beep, he'd noticed the fresh mud on the sidewalk. But hadn't given it more than a moment's notice.

But he realized now that it was mud from his shoes.

At the time he'd been too groggy to care that his shoes were muddy. But now he had to wonder how he'd gotten mud on them. The whole path he'd planned on running was paved.

Unless he *had* gone into the forest.

Julian crept to the entry hall and inspected the soles of his running shoes. They were caked with still-drying mud.

So I walked around in the trees for a while. Big deal.

Julian realized he was bargaining with the guilt rising in the pit of his stomach. He had no memory of what he had done and no reason to be in the forest.

So what was he to do now?

He was tired, and he had work in the morning. The digital clock on the microwave read 12:08.

Strike that. I have work this *morning. Guess I should sleep on it.*

But curiosity had always been Julian's besetting vice. The urge to go back to where he'd parked and hunt for clues proved overwhelming. Maybe some shoe prints would lead him back to wherever he had wandered. He wouldn't go back into the forest; not yet. Maybe next weekend.

For now, he'd just take a look around.

TH_EE

I'LL JUST LOOK around for a few minutes, Julian told himself. *See if anything's out of place. Then I'll head straight home.*

He couldn't afford to get fired from his warehouse gig, and his boss didn't like him, so calling off was out of the question.

Val would kill me if I got fired.

But he just had to satisfy his curiosity, even if he still didn't know what he was looking for.

Julian had stopped by a convenience store and bought a small flashlight and a Red Bull. Now he pulled onto the road leading to the baseball field parking lot where he'd woken up.

He mulled over where he wanted to search first. *Maybe check the bathroom where I changed or retrace the paved path for my muddy shoe prints.*

Red and blue lights strobed up ahead. Julian brushed them off as a cop catching a speeder until he noticed police units flanking the road and crowding the parking lot. Six or more officers with flashlights milled about the normally deserted lot.

Julian's brakes shrieked as he slammed them to make a U-turn. His car hit the opposite curb and jumped it. He struggled to get back in the travel lane without damaging his beater's front bumper, made it back on the road, and tried to drive off. But two rapid chirps from a police cruiser that had rolled up behind him dropped his heart into the pit of his stomach.

Julian pulled into a gravel lot a half mile from the park. Low-grade anxious under normal circumstances, he was sweating when the officer approached his window and shone an intense light in his face. He cut the engine, lowered the window, and spotted another officer nearing the passenger side.

"License and registration," the first officer stated.

"Yes, s-sir." Julian fumbled in his sweatpants pocket for his wallet.

"Slowly," the other cop ordered. "Keep your hands where I can see them."

Making every attempt to control his shaking hands, Julian got a hold of his wallet. But it stubbornly refused to let him pull it from his pocket.

"Why are you sweating so much, son?" the first cop asked in an even sterner tone than his partner's.

Julian yanked the wallet out and blurted, "Sorry, sir, I'm just a little nervous. I haven't been pulled over that much."

"What are you doing out so late? Why are you all the way out here?"

"I, I couldn't sleep, so I went for a drive," Julian said, fumbling for his license.

It wasn't in its clear plastic slot.

His favorite coffee shop's punch card still was, but nothing else.

"Sorry, Officer," Julian rambled. "I'm having trouble finding it. My license, I mean. I usually ..."

He flipped through his wallet like a clumsy stage magician, spilling cards in his lap.

"Sir," the first cop said, "I'm gonna need you to go ahead and step out of your vehicle."

"But, let me get my registration." Julian leaned toward the glove compartment.

"I told you, hands where I could see them," the second officer barked.

Julian froze and put both his hands on the wheel. He managed to exit his vehicle without further incident. The cops led him to the front of their cruiser, when a staticky blare of words came over the first officer's radio.

"Watch him," he told his partner before moving off a few feet.

Through the fear clouding his brain, Julian sensed the growing suspicion in the officer's voice as he answered the radio.

"No, nothing yet, but we just—"

Unintelligible chatter droned from the speaker.

"I see," the officer said. "Going into the woods?"

He paused for the reply.

"Well, I'll give him the option."

Julian's mind raced. *Give* what *option to* who?

"Yeah, Judge Warren is who I'd go with. The old owl might still be up." The cop signed off and walked back to Julian. "Well, Mr. ..."

"Gutierrez. Julian Gutierrez."

"Mr. Gutierrez, we've got a bit of an issue. See, you driving without a license—and that illegal U-turn you pulled—that's enough to take you into the precinct."

"But—"

The officer motioned Julian to silence. "Now, I'm sure your license just got misplaced. We'll take all your information and get this sorted out." He raised an eyebrow. "Unless we find outstanding warrants or a suspended license or something."

"No," Julian sputtered. "Nothing like that, Officer."

"Right. Now we also have to deal with the fact that you just drove kinda suspiciously by a possible crime scene. But like I said, you'll probably get off with a warning after we have your information—and we search your vehicle."

Julian opened his mouth to protest but thought better of it. *Should I let them? I got nothing to hide, but ...*"

The first policeman, Deputy Mertz, from the gold nameplate on his chest, gave him a few more seconds to think before saying "Look, it's getting searched one way or the other. Your suspicious driving is probable cause. We can take you in, and by the time you're processed and paying a fine, we'll have a search warrant. Or, you can save yourself and us a bunch of time and headaches, and just let us take a look."

In the tense silence that followed, Julian looked from Mertz' stoic expression to his partner's more hostile face. With a nod, Julian mumbled "Yeah. Go ahead, I guess." He handed Mertz his keys.

The other cop, Deputy Pulaski by *his* nameplate, motioned for Julian to follow him to the side of the cruiser. Pulaski handcuffed him, though with his hands in front. "Just a precaution," he said as he bent down to type at his dash-mounted laptop.

Against me making another run for it.

Mertz was popping the trunk of Julian's Corolla when Pulaski asked him, "Are you employed?"

"Yes, sir. I work at Connell's Furniture Warehouse. Loading and receiving."

Another cruiser pulled alongside them, and Julian sensed a shift in the atmosphere. Pulaski's radio blipped. He looked up from his laptop to a newly arrived cop. This officer was gesturing in a way that didn't sit well with Julian, though at the moment he couldn't say why. His eyes flicked down to Pulaski, who answered the newcomer with the slightest nod. Though the Deputy kept typing, his posture told Julian that something was up.

Mertz strolled from Julian's car toward Pulaski, leaving the Corolla's trunk open. His nonchalance was a put-on, as evidenced by another cop coming around the back of the cruiser Julian was leaning on.

That was when Julian knew he was in it deep. He didn't know what *it* was, but cops didn't surround you like wary hunters converging on a cornered animal for the hell of it.

The other cops approached to within five feet of Julian. Pulaski stood up beside him and said, "Mr. Gutierrez, I'm going to need you to turn around. Slowly."

"Why? What's the matter? I haven't done anything wrong."

"Just do as I say. Calmly, please."

An inner warning that the other cops were just waiting for him to do something stupid made Julian turn around.

"Hold your arms out," Mertz told him. Julian did, and

Mertz re-cuffed the prisoner's wrists behind his back.

"Julian Gutierrez, you have the right to remain silent …"

FOU_

From the *Virginia Telegraph*, October 25, 2012:

A Spotsylvania man was taken into custody today on suspicion of the kidnapping, murder, and mutilation of missing George Mason University student Kayla Reynolds. Julian R. Gutierrez, 23, was arrested early this morning by the Spotsylvania Sheriff's office with the assistance of the Virginia Highway Patrol.

According to the press conference held by Spotsylvania County Sheriff Walter Neal on Wednesday afternoon, Gutierrez was spotted driving erratically near a location where police were investigating an anonymous tip called into the hotline set up by the Reynolds family.

Reynolds, 20, was a Sophomore at GMU, studying biomedical engineering. Her disappearance, which has garnered national attention, sparked a search in the northern Virginia/D.C. area after she failed to show up to class on Monday, October 15. A subsequent search of her apartment revealed signs of a forced entry and possible kidnapping, along with several missing personal items.

Family and friends had held out hope that Reynolds would

still be found alive, despite evidence of foul play at the hands of an unknown perpetrator. But police confirmed the recovery of her body in the early daylight hours from woods adjoining the Spotsylvania Courthouse Battlefield, a Civil War National Military Park.

Reynolds was a Richmond native who graduated from Richmond Community High School in 2011 with honors. She had planned to pursue a medical degree after graduating from George Mason University.

In a statement posted on the "Bring Kayla Home" Facebook page, Reynolds' parents and siblings stated:

It is with sorrowful hearts that our darkest suspicions were confirmed, and that our beautiful daughter and sister has been taken. May the Lord accept her into His loving embrace, and may justice be delivered. We ask that the media and public at large respect our request for privacy in our time of grieving. Thank you and God Bless.

Arraignment hearings have not yet been scheduled for Gutierrez, who is currently being held at the Spotsylvania County Jail.

From the *Virginia Telegraph*, October 29, 2012:

The man arrested for the murder of George Mason University student Kayla Reynolds was arraigned today in Spotsylvania County district court. Spotsylvania resident Julian Gutierrez, 23, was charged with first-degree murder, desecration of a human corpse, concealment of a dead body, kidnapping, and providing false testimony to authorities.

Gutierrez pleaded not guilty to these charges, and his attorney requested he be allowed a reasonable bail, citing Gutierrez's clean criminal record and low flight risk.

Prosecutors objected to this request, referring to an incident Gutierrez was involved in as a minor as well as the seriousness of the charges as reasons to deny bail altogether. Judge Denise Haddock agreed bail would be denied, and the defendant would be held in the Spotsylvania County jail until further notice.

Reynolds' family was at the arraignment, as were dozens of friends and classmates, who remembered her fondly.

"Kay was such a sweet girl," Kayla's close friend Angela Mazzetti told the *Telegraph*. "Just someone that everyone loved being around, and someone I could always go to when I was having any problem or just needed to talk. I still can't believe she was taken from us. We were supposed to go to medical school together, and now that's never going to happen."

Though her parents and close family were in attendance, they chose not to speak to the media, but instead released a statement through a family attorney.

"We are grateful for the efforts of the police that they were able to apprehend Kayla's abductor so quickly. We are heartbroken to know that she died in such a cruel and violent way, and can only pray that God's justice is swift. We also pray that the justice system delivers an appropriate punishment to the man who perpetrated her death. Our Kayla deserves that, as she was such a light and that it is such a sin that that light was extinguished at such an early age."

According to an affidavit signed by arresting officer Edward Mertz, Gutierrez was seen driving past the parking lot near the Spotsylvania Civil War memorial in the early morning hours last Thursday. Police had been alerted to suspicious activity in the area via an anonymous tip. As police units from Spotsylvania County and the Virginia Highway Patrol were investigating, Gutierrez's car proceeded to do a U-turn past the scene. Gutierrez reportedly attempted to flee before being pulled over by Mertz.

Mertz described Gutierrez as nervous and somewhat uncooperative and noted that he failed to produce a driver's license when asked. After observing this unusual behavior, Mertz asked for permission to search Gutierrez's vehicle, which Gutierrez gave.

What that search yielded is sealed pending further investigation, but police say there is evidence tying some contents of Gutierrez's vehicle to the site where Reynolds' body was found.

The affidavit made no mention of motive or a previous connection between Gutierrez and the victim.

From *The Beltway Tribune*, June 23, 2014:

The trial of a Spotsylvania man accused of murder began today, almost two years after the body of his alleged victim, a George Mason University student, was found in a wooded area on the outskirts of Fredericksburg in northern Virginia.

The disappearance and murder of Richmond native Kayla Reynolds captured national attention in the fall of 2012. And the subsequent arrest of her alleged killer has many in the area, especially Reynolds' loved ones and friends, clamoring for closure.

Julian Gutierrez, 25, is accused of kidnapping Reynolds from her apartment in Fairfax in October of 2012. Police found her mutilated remains a week later, partly buried near the Spotsylvania Courthouse Battlefield national park.

Opening arguments began with the prosecution outlining its

case. Prosecutor James Allen Kincaid asserted that Gutierrez followed Ms. Reynolds to her apartment and forced entry to sexually assault her. Though there was no evidence of rape, he alleged that the defendant knocked Reynolds unconscious and carried her body to his vehicle. Gutierrez then drove to an unknown location where he killed Reynolds and dismembered her body. He then drove to the remote wooded area outside the Spotsylvania city limits where he buried her body in an attempt to hide the evidence of her murder.

Kincaid described how evidence, including rope whose fibers matched those discovered on Reynolds' body, and chloroform reported in her autopsy, were both found in the trunk of Gutierrez's car.

Incredibly, Gutierrez was caught driving by the crime scene about an hour after an anonymous tip directed police to the location. The defendant's erratic driving and suspicious behavior caught investigating officers' attention. Their subsequent search of Gutierrez's car turned up the incriminating evidence.

In his opening statement, the defendant's lawyer Kerry Conway spun a different story. Repeatedly insisting that his client did not know and had never been in contact with the victim, Conway dismissed all evidence linking the two as completely circumstantial. The counsel for the defense even implied that police had planted the rope and chloroform to frame Mr. Gutierrez. Conway stated that his client could not have kidnapped or murdered Ms. Reynolds and accused police of building a "case of convenience" against Gutierrez that let the actual killer go free.

After opening statements, the prosecution introduced several items as evidence, including rope found at the forest scene where Reynolds' body had been partly buried, as well as three bottles of chloroform. One of those bottles was found broken under the victim's body. Also submitted were blood-soaked rags confirmed by forensics experts to contain DNA from both Reynolds and Gutierrez, as well as a GPS watch belonging to Gutierrez.

As its first witness, the prosecution called the arresting officer, Spotsylvania County Deputy Edward Mertz. Deputy Mertz testified that Gutierrez drove by the parking lot scene early on the morning of October 25, 2012. Located near woods bordering the battlefield park, the lot lies approximately four miles from where Reynolds' body was found. Mertz further testified that he had been notified of suspicious activity in the area by a call to the tip line set up by Reynolds' family.

Mertz said that when the defendant's car approached within sight of the scene, it performed a sudden U-turn and attempted to speed away. Mertz and his partner Anthony Pulaski pulled Gutierrez over a short distance from the parking lot. When the accused could not produce his driver's license, Mertz ordered him out of the vehicle and instructed him to give his information to Pulaski.

Deputy Mertz testified that he was informed via radio that officers at the parking lot scene had found a suspected blood trail and footprints leading from the woods to one of the parking spaces. He asked Gutierrez for permission to search his vehicle, to which the defendant gave.

The prosecution asked the Deputy if he had probable cause for a search. Mertz said he did, citing the defendant's erratic driving, the scene's remote location, and Gutierrez's nervous manner. Asked why the defendant would agree to a search if he knew there was incriminating evidence the in trunk, Mertz said, "You'll have to ask him why."

On cross-examination, the defense pressed Deputy Mertz about whether he had probable cause to pull the defendant over or search his vehicle. The Deputy insisted that proper procedure had been followed, noting that the defendant's vehicle had gone over the opposite curb, constituting failure to maintain a travel lane, which gave cause to pull a driver over. Further, considering the seriousness of the crime, not investigating a suspicious vehicle would have been negligent. Mertz elaborated that had nothing suspicious been found in the defendant's vehicle, he would likely have gotten off with a minor citation for driving without a license.

Asked if Mertz had threatened to take the defendant to jail if he refused the search, Mertz said, "Absolutely not."

From *The Beltway Tribune*, July 1, 2014:

The Kayla Reynolds murder trial entered its seventh day this morning. Prosecutors called Dr. Karen MacIntyre, a forensic pathologist with the FBI, to the stand. Her presentation of Ms. Reynolds' fatal injuries and the mutilation of the victim's body upset many in the courtroom.

A notable exception was defendant Julian Gutierrez. The accused simply lowered his eyes as MacIntyre presented crime scene photos showing the postmortem amputation of Reynolds' arms and legs. He sat expressionless as MacIntyre described how the victim's limbs and torso had been bound with rope and wrapped in heavy plastic for partial burial in the woods near the scene of the defendant's arrest.

Asked by the prosecution how Ms. Reynolds had died, MacIntyre stated that the victim had been stabbed seven times in the upper back and neck, most likely bleeding out from those injuries.

MacIntyre could only speculate about where the killing took place. She did cite the relative lack of blood in the plastic wrappings and the shallow grave as grounds for casting doubt on the burial site as the murder scene.

"So, he killed her at some unknown location, dismembered her as your report describes, and then transported her body to the forest, is what you're saying?" Prosecutor James Allen Kincaid asked MacIntyre.

"Yes, that's what the evidence tells us happened," the forensics expert answered.

Kincaid further questioned Dr. MacIntyre about the rope and fibers found in the defendant's vehicle, as well as on the clothes he was wearing the night of his arrest. She confirmed that both sets of fibers were identical to those of the rope binding Reynolds' body parts together. Asked to elaborate, Dr. MacIntyre explained that the ends of the rope at the forest scene and the fragments in the car had matched up perfectly. In addition, a knife found in the defendant's car was conclusively identified as the blade that had cut the rope.

On cross-examination, defense counsel Kerry Conway repeatedly brought up the presence of DNA not belonging to the victim or Mr. Gutierrez. Dr. MacIntyre acknowledged the discovery of additional DNA but testified that no match could be found in any national crime database. MacIntyre theorized that cross-contamination could have introduced DNA from people with whom the victim or defendant had been in close proximity.

Asked to clarify, Dr. MacIntyre explained that an associate of Mr. Gutierrez could have come into contact with the rope, the bag, or the jars of chloroform, inadvertently transferring DNA onto those objects.

Conway questioned why police had not conjectured that an accomplice may have been involved in, or another perpetrator entirely responsible for, these crimes. But Judge Haddock agreed with Kincaid's objection and struck down the defense's argument as speculation. Dr. MacIntyre reiterated that cross-contamination was the most likely explanation, citing that small amounts of investigators' DNA were also found on pieces of evidence.

Edward Reynolds, the victim's father—and the only family member in attendance—stated afterward, "I didn't want my family to have to go through this, to have to hear and see what this butcher did to her. But I was here, I needed to be there for my little girl. She deserved so much better and I wasn't going to let that animal think for a second that her family was ever going to forget."

From *The Beltway Tribune*, July 18, 2014:

Closing arguments in the trial of Julian Gutierrez for the 2012 murder of Kayla Reynolds began today, marking the close of the four-week proceedings.

The prosecution began by detailing how they believed Gutierrez, whom coworkers characterized as a loner with few friends and no romantic relationships, began stalking Reynolds in the weeks before her disappearance. They argued that his obsession took a deadly turn on the night of October 12 when he kidnapped, killed, and dismembered the victim, disposing of her in a wooded part of the Spotsylvania Courthouse Battlefield.

Lead prosecutor James Allen Kincaid recounted the extensive physical evidence tying Mr. Gutierrez to the crime scene. This evidence included rope fragments and fibers identical to the rope found at the shallow grave where Ms. Reynolds' body was buried. Traces of the victim's blood found along with chloroform bottles in the trunk of the defendant's car, Kincaid argued, pointed to Gutierrez as the sole culprit.

Kincaid also reviewed the evidence retrieved from the defendant's watch. The device's GPS proved that Gutierrez had walked to the crime scene only hours before an anonymous tip called police to the area.

The prosecution closed by reminding the jury of the brutality Reynolds must have suffered in her last moments and the indignity with which her killer had treated her body afterward. Kincaid urged the jury of 8 women and 4 men to not only convict Gutierrez on all counts, but to give him the death sentence for the cruel manner in which he had ended Kayla Reynolds' life.

During its closing arguments, the defense attempted to undermine the prosecution's case on several fronts. First, it cited the lack of any evidence that the defendant had even known of, much less stalked, the victim at any point. Defense attorney Kerry Conway cast doubt on the defendant's ability to physically transport the victim unnoticed, given the security at her apartment complex and Gutierrez's small stature.

Conway then reviewed the defendant's cell phone records for the day Reynolds went missing. Tracking data showed that on the day in question the phone had remained forty-five miles away in Fredericksburg, where the defendant had then resided. And several calls had been placed to and from the phone during that time.

Conway also questioned the validity of the GPS data gleaned from Gutierrez's watch, as well as the prosecution's "razor-thin attempt at a motive." He closed by stating "There are millions of lonely young men in America. Their loneliness alone is a not a motivation for murder, and it is a farce to attempt to apply it to Julian Gutierrez in this case."

Upon rebuttal, the prosecution reminded the jury that the defendant could have simply left his phone in Fredericksburg during the kidnapping—by accident or otherwise. "Just because his phone was in Fredericksburg doesn't mean he was with it," said Kincaid.

From *The Beltway Tribune*, July 23, 2014:

After only 14 hours of deliberation the jury in the trial of Julian Gutierrez returned with a verdict of guilty on all counts. They further imposed the death penalty for his murder of Kayla Reynolds.

Shouts of joy erupted from the gallery, where many of Reynolds' family and friends had assembled, when the jury foreperson read the verdict.

"Justice has been done, by God," Reynolds' father Edward said through tears with his family gathered around him. "It has been done. Our daughter, our little girl can finally rest."

Gutierrez merely lowered his head as the verdict was read, showing little emotion, though tears could also be seen on his face. A small contingent of his family members reached out and hugged him before he was led away by court bailiffs.

Along with first-degree murder, Gutierrez was also convicted of kidnapping, desecration of a human corpse, concealment of a dead body, and providing false testimony to authorities.

This conviction marks the outcome of a two-year legal battle to bring Kayla Reynolds' killer to justice. An appeal is expected.

Gutierrez is to be held at the Sussex I State Prison on death row.

_IVE

I TURN THIRTY today.
Not that it matters.
Not in this place.

There behind dank walls, hard metal, and harder people, birthdays, holidays—even seasons, didn't mean shit.

Calendars only mattered to Real People living Out There.

Only Julian's sister, one of the few people on the outside who remembered he was alive, had visited him. He'd never had many friends, and the few losers he'd hung around with were busy pretending they'd never known him.

Not that they were model citizens. A couple of them had beat up a bum in Richmond when he was fifteen. And because Julian was with them when they were arrested, he got charged with abetting.

That charge was supposed to have been sealed when he turned eighteen. But the prosecution had still brought it up at his trial. *Look everyone, look at this career criminal that helped kick the shit out of a homeless person, he's killing young women now! Lock him up, put him down like a rabid dog!*

Having nothing but time, he'd read plenty of stories about guys convicted of murder, rape, or other atrocities that had been exonerated later. Most of them were more thankful than angry.

But most of those guys had been in the joint for decades. They were in their forties or fifties and happy just to have a little life left to live Out There.

Julian guessed he just hadn't stewed in his own private hell long enough to forgive. He was still angry, though his was a solemn anger.

His sister Val had always seen through his stoic front, even when they were kids. And she'd never been one to let him keep brooding.

"What's with the sad eyes, *hombre?*" her tinny voice asked him through the plexiglass divider over a cracked telephone handset.

She'd always been the strong one, the one he looked up to even though she was barely over five feet. He looked at her now, dark hair like their mom's, kind but intense eyes like their dad's, and it made him sad. Sad that she'd had to make so many sacrifices for him.

"Don't you mean 'Happy birthday,' Sis?"

"I was getting to that. But first turn that frown upside down, *cabrón.*"

He flashed a brief but genuine smile for her. Val and her husband Calvin were the last of his visitors. A cousin from out-of-state had come to see him a while back. He wasn't even sure if it had been that year or last.

His parents would have visited if they hadn't died in a car accident years ago, leaving Val to raise him.

She'd done her best.

"So, happy birthday, Julian. Sorry Cal and the kids couldn't be here. He's got a work thing, and the kids, they're all sick with some flu or something. I got a girlfriend looking after them. So, what's going on with you?"

She's always like this.

It didn't matter that her brother was on death row, that the prison smelled like piss and mold and desperation. Never mind that it was a weekend after her night shift at the hospital. Despite Val's sunny disposition, the bags under her eyes betrayed her exhaustion. But she always spoke to him like they were catching up over lunch.

He would be pissed if anyone other than his sister gave him

such a cheery attitude. But she'd always been there, fighting for him. She'd sold a car and put a lien against her house just to hire his lawyer.

Not that it had mattered.

Conway had advised him from the start to take the plea deal. He'd get life, though maybe get out in forty years or so, but the death penalty would be taken off the table.

Julian had refused.

He was innocent.

That meant something in America, right?

Yeah. It means fuck all.

Val could *still* be paying for his lawyer; she'd never mention it. He'd asked her husband during one of his sister's rare absences. But Calvin was just as tight-lipped about it.

So Julian just smiled at his sister; told her about the latest book he'd read and a little about the project he was thinking of writing.

He ran out of things to say, and she fell silent. The desperation to fill their limited time with idle words pressed down on him.

"Why are you still in Virginia?" Julian blurted.

The question had been weighing on his mind for a while, but the moment he said it, he regretted it. Seeing Val's always-composed face fall hurt his heart.

"What kind of question is that, Julian? What the hell?"

Against his better judgment he said, "I know you always wanted to go back west, like to Colorado or the Oregon coast, right? Like when we were little kids before dad got the job out here? Sis, I'm gonna be dead in a couple years anyway, so why are you still here?"

"You selfish son of a bitch, you—" She burst out crying for the first time since their parents' funeral.

Julian lowered his eyes to the graffiti-etched counter. "Sis …"

Val dropped the handset. Despite the plexiglass divider going all the way up to the ceiling, her sobs bled across to him. Julian took some comfort from the fact that he was the only inmate with a visitor. And the guard behind him didn't care or at least pretended not to. That was good. Letting someone else see her cry would just piss his sister off. So Julian just waited quietly, his eyes welling up in the meantime.

After a few minutes, Val composed herself and wiped her eyes with her blouse sleeve. She picked up the handset and got back to business. "What if you get a commuted sentence? Or a federal appeal?"

Julian stared back at her. "So what, Val? I'll still be in here. And I'm not getting another appeal. There's too much evidence saying I'm the guy. Shit, remember that Innocence Project letter we got?"

She opened her mouth as if to object further but stayed silent. The letter had used a lot of flowery language, but they could have cut the crap and just said, "We don't deal with people we know are guilty."

At last, Val said, "Then who's going to visit you, huh? You just going to be the tough guy and go it alone?"

He nodded. "Yeah, I guess. Once I'm gone, you'll be one of the few people who ever knew me. I don't matter anymore, Val."

"What about your poetry, *pendejo*? What about that book you're writing? I got half of it proofread already. You gonna make me finish it myself?"

"Val—"

"Yeah, I *will* finish it. And I'll make that main character of yours a little-dicked crybaby who needs some *chichona* to come along and slaps some manliness into him." She smiled a little through fresh tears.

Julian couldn't help but crack a faint smile of his own. With a quivering voice he said, "OK, I'm sorry. You know I love and appreciate you. But I don't want you putting things on hold for me. Your kids should know their family."

"*You're* their family. They'll know you for as long as you're here."

"OK. I'm sorry. And thanks for the birthday visit."

"The kids are already planning a big party for your next

one. At our place. It's supposed to be a secret, so act surprised, OK?"

Julian gave a harsh laugh. "You shouldn't lead them on like that."

Val set her jaw. "Maybe next year is a bit optimistic. Or even the year after that. But one day we'll be celebrating with you on the outside. Just wait and see."

The Mousetrap Manifesto - The Defective

THE MOUSETRAP MURDERS us all.

This is a confession of the Fulcrum:

Alastor remembered when the ideas of his greatness and of the Mousetrap began. It was before he found the book, before he began germinating the Fulcrum. It started when he went to the hillside where he sat watching the road.
    He grew up the oldest of three children in a Tennessee nothing town filled with ignorant nothing people. When he was twelve, his father had died in the war. Not that he cared if his father was dead. Charlie St. John had been an insolent, violent man who would beat his wife and children whenever the mood took him.
    One of his last memories of the man was when Alastor's youngest brother Todd was only two, their father had hit him for being fussy about eating. So ol' Charlie had shipped out one day soon after and got himself fragged by a mortar in the evacuation. At least that's what the young soldier who'd visited them said.
    All they got back was a folded-up flag his mother kept in a drawer somewhere. Alastor didn't know if the Fulcrum could have been formed with his father around. Maybe that's what

their preacher had meant when he'd rattled on about Providence.

In his father's absence, Alastor only had his mother to contend with. It was bearable since she spent most of her time drinking herself into oblivion. And he spent most of his time wandering the nearby woods.

It was on one of those outings—a walk to the hillside—when thoughts about the power he could have if he just reached out and grabbed it formed in his young mind.

The hillside gave him the perfect vantage on the one road leading into town. And the roadkill. He would sit for hours on that hillside watching squirrels, raccoons, and even deer go from recognizable animals to red-gray smears on the blacktop. Sometimes he would walk down and reposition carcasses that got knocked off the roadside.

This close observation gave him an epiphany about what an inane concept life was. One minute you were a functioning machine, and the next just a thing, an object to be thrown away.

But within the inanity he found the power of life and death. He could remove one and replace it with the other. That revelation evoked more wonder than any rambling sermon he'd sat through.

He also realized that death held a special place in society. People gave those surrounded by death special treatment. For a few weeks after his father was KIA, people had been kinder to Alastor. That had been the only real gift ol' Charlie had ever given him.

Not that he cared. Most of the classmates who gave him forced smiles were idiots, backward hill folk who talked too loud and thought too little.

Except for one.

Lisa Pembry.

Alastor had always liked her: a sweet little blonde girl who sang at church and always wore a ribbon in her hair. After his father was killed, she had been real sweet to Alastor; even hugged him once. One Sunday, he'd looked on as Lisa bent over to tie her shoe. When they got home, his mother, who had noticed him notice Lisa, had told him he had a devil in him and rubbed soap in his eyes. She forbade him from being around Lisa after that.

And that was his mother's gift. He had gotten caught; there'd been consequences.

So he learned not to get caught.

He took to hiding in the shadows, glimpsing forbidden pleasures—including Lisa—whenever he could.

Alastor wasn't mad at his mother. He had always despised her and the way she lived. But he wasn't mad.

His smoldering hatred was reserved for someone else.

Gary Hankinson was a defective, a mental retard. The boys called him Gay Weed because the idiot couldn't even say his own name right. He would slobber on himself when he was trying to read in class and always had crumbs on his shirt.

But for some reason most of the girls in the class, especially Lisa, like to help Gary out. She would sit with him sometimes and read the words out loud as he dragged his sausage finger across the page. She would even wipe his disgusting chin as he laughed and hugged her.

Alastor had never been the jealous kind, but he hated that Gary had Lisa's eye.

He found a solution one summer morning while watching roadkill from his hill.

Lisa had a Cocker Spaniel named Peaches. It was a useless animal in Alastor's eyes, no good for hunting or working on a farm. But Lisa loved on it the way she loved on Gay Weed.

As Alastor watched for a car to cruise by and further flatten a raccoon splayed at the tip of a yellow line, two ideas smashed together: the power of death, and not getting caught.

One would rip Lisa away from that stupid dog. The other would rip Gay Weed away from Lisa.

Alastor mulled it over all night and thought up a simple solution.

From his skulking, he knew that the Pembrys kept their dog in the backyard, and the stupid thing came right up to anyone that passed by. Alastor also knew that Gay Weed lived on the edge of town less than a mile from him.

Late one night Alastor snuck out of his room with some scraps of jerky. He coaxed the dumb mutt to him while the Pembry family slept. The dog started yelping when he picked it up, but he was already a big boy, strong enough to force its mouth shut. He ran back home and locked the dog in a shed far behind the house until the next morning.

Then he got his stuff together and kept watch on Gay Weed. Just like as if he was back at his hillside, watching for a big, dumb raccoon to come along.

Gary played in his backyard with a wooden train as his mother gardened. Just before noon, she finally went inside. Gay Weed stayed, still pushing the little kid's toy in the dirt.

Alastor stepped from the woods behind the property. "Hey, Gary."

The defective boy looked up to see who had called his name. His vacant eyes showed no recognition.

"It's me, Alastor. You know, from school."

That stupid infuriating grin spread on Gary's fat cheeks, making Alastor anxious to rid himself of the thing. He held up a candy in its wrapper, and the toy train was forgotten.

Making sure he wasn't noticed, Alastor led the imbecile into the woods. He had already tied the spaniel to a tree, and a shallow rut indicated it had worked itself back and forth. The rope had dug into the tree's bark and the dog's neck, leaving the skin red and raw.

"Hey Gary, do you like marmalade?"

Before leaving the house, Alastor had gone down to the cellar and swiped a jar. His mother hadn't made preserves since the alcohol had laid waste to her. The shelves once stocked with peach jam and apple butter were almost bare, but he had found the marmalade.

He had also stolen a bottle of his mother's whiskey. Alastor mixed a spoonful with the spread and offered it to Gary. The stupid boy ate it greedily and reached for the jar.

Alastor jerked the preserves back and offered the bottle.

"You have to drink first."

Gary took a sip from the bottle. His wide mouth puckered as if about to spew the whiskey out.

"I'll finish this whole jar myself if you don't swallow," Alastor warned.

Gary forced the liquor down. Alastor poured more into the jar and handed it over.

Gay Weed ate and ate in the sweltering Tennessee afternoon. After a while, his eyes went half-lidded. "Don't like it."

"You're almost done, Gary. Finish up the jar, and I'll let you go down there and pet that dog. You wanna pet it, don't ya?"

Gay Weed's slobbery lips bent in a worried frown, but Alastor was already learning how to both intimidate and manipulate people. And the half-wit made it easy. "C'mon, Gary, we want to go pet that doggie, don't we?"

The stupid boy nodded and scooped another spoonful into his doughy mouth.

Twenty minutes later, the marmalade-caked idiot lay dozing.

Alastor walked to a pile of branches under a nearby tree. He'd been helping the old widow down the street tidy up her yard since her husband's passing last year. And he'd taken the .22 Marlin he'd found leaning in a corner of the garage—along with two boxes of ammo.

Clearing away the branch pile uncovered the stolen lever action rifle. Alastor skulked back to Gay Weed, sat down next to him, and trained the Marlin's sights on the dog. It thrashed back and forth, choking itself in its struggle to get loose.

Only eight rounds remained of the original two boxes, so Alastor took his time. The first shot missed high, splintering bark just above where he'd tied the rope. The dog ignored the sharp crack and kept pulling.

He shot again. The dog yelped as the bullet caught it in the ribs. Alastor chambered another round and fired quick. The dog slumped to the ground.

Alastor cast an expressionless glance at Gay Weed, who still lay sticky and motionless.

He wasn't looking forward to the next part, but it had to be done.

Alastor levered another round into the chamber, turned the rifle around, and pressed the still-hot muzzle to the meaty part of his triceps. He gritted his teeth, took a deep breath, and pulled the trigger with his thumb. He yelled as the bullet ripped through an inch of skin and meat. The blood gushing out was a concern, but the pain was bearable. He could finish the job.

He punched the unconscious idiot hard in the face. With any luck a bruise would be forming by the time anyone showed up. Alastor next placed the rifle in Gary's hands, making sure the imbecile's finger was in the trigger guard. Then he broke into a run toward the road. He waited, bleeding, for a while before stepping into the open and flagging down the first car he saw.

The police found Gary Hankinson in the woods, where he had apparently tied up the Pembrys' beloved dog Peaches and shot it to death.

Alastor told the Sheriff he'd heard the shooting and the dog yelping. When he'd gone to see what was going on, Gary had shot him in the arm. He said he'd knocked Gary out, despite being shot, and made a run for it. Thank heaven he'd come upon Mr. Anders driving down the road.

They'd packed Gay Weed off to a state hospital or some damn place.

Alastor didn't see Lisa again, not even at church, until school started again. She was different, though. He thought that maybe if he caught a dog and gave it to her, she would cheer up. But her family moved away soon after, which Alastor thought was probably for the best.

He had gotten what he needed from the experience.

He understood the power of death.

And knew that if he was smart and patient enough, he could get away with anything.

Part II: The Breadcrumb Trail

When life has rolled you over
Making mince of bones and all
When the night is dark and starless
The day, an obsidian caul

Give a thought to those damned wretches
Born of neither name nor gift
And ever should you Remember
Even the mighty Sun is a soul adrift
-The Death Row Inmate

S_X

JULIAN GOT THE postcard two weeks after his birthday. It read:

> *Mr. Gutierrez, my name is Raymond Bendall. You don't know me, but I've spent the last seven years thinking about you and what you must have gone through. What you're still going through. I'm so sorry that I didn't contact you sooner, before the trial, because maybe I could have made a difference.*
>
> *To be honest I wasn't in any condition to help anyone back then. I was homeless at the time and strung out pretty bad.*
>
> *But that is no excuse.*
>
> *I should have gone to someone, the police or a priest maybe, and let them know what I know.*
>
> *Mr. Gutierrez, I know you didn't kill that girl.*
>
> *I know because I saw who did.*
>
> *You were there, but not really, and I know you're not a murderer.*

A signature was scrawled at the end of the message, almost indiscernible in stark contrast to the neatly typed body. The front of the postcard bore a landscape with Monticello in the background and a pink cursive graphic proclaiming "Virginia is for Lovers!"

Julian didn't know what to do with the postcard at first. He thought maybe it was a sick joke, someone playing a prank on him. It had happened before. But this Raymond Bendall guy had left his address and a phone number.

The prison staff weren't supposed to read inmates' mail, just search it for contraband and skim for signs of illegal activity. But Julian didn't want to take any chances. He copied Bendall's message word-for-word into a letter and sent it to his sister.

Maybe she'll be able to contact the guy, maybe get a lawyer to investigate or something.

Or at least find out what the hell "You were there, but not really" meant.

But the phrase that kept Julian up that night was "I know you're not a murderer." It kindled the tiniest hope of proving he wasn't the monster that everyone—even, he suspected, Val —was convinced he was.

I know you're not a murderer.

SE_EN

VAL CALLED THE number Julian gave her and spoke to Bendall's mother. The woman, whose voice placed her in her fifties or sixties, gave the distinct impression she wasn't too pleased about being contacted.

"Raymond's not well," his mother demurred.

"My brother is on death row," Val explained. "Your son claims to have information that could exonerate him."

The old woman clicked her tongue. "If you absolutely must speak with him, it would be best if you came to the house."

So Val found herself parking her old Honda Civic in front of a house in a depressed part of Fredericksburg. She'd heard no deceit in the old woman's voice and doubted she was in danger. Even so, she didn't like the idea of going into a strange house alone. Cal had offered to come, but they'd been unable to find a sitter on short notice.

The small can of pepper spray at her hip provided some comfort in her husband's absence.

Val got out of the car, climbed the Bendall's front steps, and knocked.

"Who's there?" a familiar voice rasped from behind the small, smudged window set in the scuffed pine door.

"I'm Valentina Cooper, Mrs. Bendall. We spoke on the phone about your son's postcard."

The door opened, and the frail-looking woman inside regarded her visitor. "You sounded White on the phone. And with the last name a' Cooper, I figured ..." She squinted. "You Puerto Rican?"

Val gave her a wry smile. "Just regular ol' Mexican. Sorry to disappoint."

The smile was not returned. "Well, come on in. Raymond's in the living room."

Val's suspicions dissolved as she stepped into the house. It was tidy, if rather cluttered with cupboards full of porcelain knickknacks and hotel lobby style paintings.

The old woman—a bit of a grouch, but not a threat—led Val through the dining room past a large oak table with a plastic-encased Washington football helmet for a centerpiece.

"Hail to the Redskins," Val said.

"I let my husband have one thing of his own in my dining room," the old woman scoffed, "and *that's* what he chooses. The moment he stops breathing, it's going in the attic."

Val cracked a smile, hoping to thaw her hostess' iciness. The old woman showed no sign it had worked.

The living room stood in stark contrast to the dining room. A flat-screen TV hung across the sparsely furnished area, showing a nature program. The volume was muted, and closed captions scrolled across the bottom of the display. Two overstuffed sofas hugged opposite walls, and at the center of the room sat a man in an electric wheelchair.

Val, a nurse practitioner, saw telltale signs of muscle atrophy in his legs and arms, although he couldn't have been older than thirty-five. His feet and hands curled inward.

He's been in this state for a while. She couldn't tell how much mobility he had, but the absence of a tracheotomy meant communication wouldn't be an issue.

The old woman gently nudged the man's shoulder. "Raymond. Raymond, honey, your visitor is here."

The man picked up the TV remote from his lap and paused the show. He turned the wheelchair with an armrest-mounted joystick to face the two women.

"Hi, Raymond," said Val. "I'm here to ask about the letter you sent my brother."

He spoke in a low, slow voice. "You're Julian's sister?"

"Yes, I'm Valentina. But you can call me Val."

The old woman in a friendlier tone now, said, "Please sit down, Miss Cooper. Can I get you some water or tea?"

"Tea will be fine, thank you."

The old woman left the room.

Val studied Raymond a bit more. His eyes looked tired but sincere. *He might have told Julian the truth!*

"She was mean to you on the phone," Raymond said.

"It's alright. I know it was a bit suspicious, me calling out of the blue."

"No, she was expecting a call. It's just that Mom is that way with everybody new."

"Expecting? Does she know about the postcard you sent?"

"Who do you think typed it?" Raymond's mother said, returning to the room. She handed Val a glass half full of ice and poured some tea from a pitcher. "Raymond's wanted to contact your brother for a year or so. At first I thought he was making it up, too."

Val took a cool sip of instant tea and undissolved granules. "Sorry if I sounded a little skeptical," she told Raymond. "Everyone's convinced my brother did it. Even I had moments of doubt about him. And no witness has ever come forward to back him up."

"No one?" Raymond's mother said.

"We get crazies every once in a while," said Val. "Attention-seekers. Or people wanting to hurt us."

Raymond met her eye. "I'm not crazy. And I couldn't hurt anyone if I wanted to."

Val cleared her throat. "At the time of the murder you weren't as ... debilitated?"

"No, I was fine physically. Just addicted to drugs. Heroin at first mostly, but I started doing meth, too. I was twenty when I saw your brother in the woods."

So he's only twenty-seven now. Sympathy tugged on Val's heart. Addiction and illness had taken their toll on the man.

"I ran away from home in high school," Raymond said.

"Made it to D.C. and lived there for a few years. It was dumb luck I didn't get myself killed. I made it back to Fred Vegas in the spring of 2012, I guess."

Val smiled a little at the mention of Fredericksburg's nickname. Raymond seemed to be coping with his ailment better than many of her own patients.

Raymond continued. "I kept to alleys and shelters here in town most of the time. But that day I was hungry and fiending for a hit because I hadn't scored anything in a while."

Raymond's head slumped, pressing his chin to his chest. Val thought he'd drifted off, but he resumed talking with his eyes closed.

"It was cold that day. I was broke, but a dealer friend from high school said he'd front me a little ice. There's this baseball field out by the Spotsylvania Civil War park that's practically abandoned in the fall. So my buddy and I picked it as a meet site.

"I was out there huddled under the bleachers when I saw someone walking around. Tall guy in a hoodie. Big. He came out of nowhere with a huge duffel bag on his shoulder."

Raymond raised his head. His face had gone pale, and his sweat-damp brow reflected the mute television's glow. "Mom, will you get me some tea?"

His mother got up and retrieved an empty glass with a straw. Val picked up the pitcher from the end table and filled Raymond's glass. The older woman gave her a grateful look and lowered the straw to Raymond's mouth.

Raymond gulped down a swig of tea and continued. "I could tell the guy wasn't right. Not that I can judge anyone, but he gave off a weird vibe, walking around a deserted park like that with a bag. He didn't see me under the bleachers. I think he would have hurt me if he had. Anyhow, he kept walking down the path a ways, and then he went into the forest."

Val leaned forward. Her fear returned, not as the vague anxiety she'd felt for herself upon entering Raymond's house, but as deep secondhand dread for him.

Raymond licked his pale lips. "The whole time I was telling myself, 'So what, some guy's walking by? What's the big deal? You're just paranoid cuz you need a fix.'

"But however much I repeated it, I couldn't believe it. So I waited till he was out of sight and snuck out to see what was up. But those woods, man—they're no joke. You can get lost, easy. I went in right where I saw him go, but pretty soon I wasn't sure where he was, and I damn sure didn't know where *I* was."

Raymond's mother squeezed his hand.

"So there I was," he went on, "lost and frantic. And it was getting late, so I figured I should retrace my steps and get the hell out of there. Whatever that guy was up to was his business, right? But after an hour or so I was still just wandering around, freaked out. The leaves crunching under my feet sounded like firecrackers popping off. I knew if I kept it up, I'd get found out. So I just lay down by a fallen log.

"I must have dozed off. Because next thing I knew, this sound like metal on metal, or metal on rock, woke me up. It was already dark. No way I was finding my way back, so I started sneaking toward whatever that sound was. Pretty soon I saw light peeking over a low ridge up ahead. I went over the ridge, real slow, and there was my man, digging a hole with a shovel in the light of a tripod lamp."

The hope flickering in Val's heart fought a sinking feeling in her stomach.

"That duffel bag lay off to the side. It was open, and ..." Raymond took another draw from his tea and fell silent.

Val held him in a gaze that may have been more intense than intended.

Raymond looked away. "I saw the plastic bag," he croaked. "Something was in there. Something too weird for me to identify. There was plenty of red, though."

"It was a body," Val said.

Raymond gave a slow nod. "I think I didn't want to admit it; not then." His chin sagged onto his chest. "That's when I noticed your brother."

Now it was Val's turn to break into a sweat. She might have suspected Raymond Bendall of pulling a prank when she first read the postcard, but unless he was Fredericksburg's finest actor, she believed he was telling the truth now.

"He was there," Raymond said, "passed out to one side and dressed like he'd been jogging. That's right, isn't it? He said he was running that day?"

Val nodded. "What about the big guy?"

"He still had that hoodie on. I couldn't see his face, but he was working hard, puffing steam from his mouth and nose; even from his head through the top of the hood. He finished the hole and put the plastic bag in.

"Here's the thing, though: There was this little box over by your brother. I didn't notice it until the guy picked it up walked into the forest with it, a flashlight, and the shovel. A few minutes later I heard more digging. Then he came back without the box. I think he buried it out there somewhere."

Was there another victim? Val wondered. *No, Raymond said the second box was small.* She puzzled over the little box's contents until Raymond spoke again.

"When the big guy got back, he took your brother and pressed his hand all over the bag, the ground next to it, and the shovel. I think Julian was drugged."

"How do you know?" asked Val.

Raymond gave a sad laugh. "Take it from an ex-junkie. Besides, he was limp as a rag doll."

"You're saying Julian's prints were planted at the scene?" Val voiced a sudden doubt. "Why didn't the cops find hoodie man's?"

"The big guy was wearing gloves," said Raymond. "After he framed your brother, he covered the hole with dirt and rocks and stuff."

"And this guy," said Val, "did he just leave? Or did he take Julian somewhere?"

Raymond sighed. "He left most everything—except that light. He turned it off and broke it down. But he had a flashlight, and he did a sweep of the area. Then he picked your brother up like a sack of potatoes and headed in my direction. I was afraid he saw me, so I just lay there praying he'd walk on by."

Tears streamed down Raymond's face as his mother caressed his head. "Thank God he did."

The Mousetrap Manifesto - Primer

THE MOUSETRAP MURDERS us all.

This is a confession of the Fulcrum:

The Fulcrum upon which this decrepit society would one day hinge required a proof of concept—proof beyond the vermin and that stupid dog.
   He required a human proof.
   At the time he was still known as Alastor St. John, a young student at Louisiana State University, and he had been waiting for his moment to prove himself.
   To accept his providence.
   But waiting had never been a problem for this most patient of men. He was eminently suited for the task, and he had accepted the burden, no matter the cost.
   As before, he observed his prey. He watched them mill about, unaware of the danger their proximity to him posed. Like sheep unwary of the predator in their midst, he could slaughter any of them he liked.
   He was already a big man and strong. "Country strong" those idiots back home said.
   What did they know? He was Providence strong and equipped with every faculty necessary to become the tool of

change he had envisioned himself as long ago.
So he waited.
He watched.
He prepared.
He especially enjoyed watching people at night, when the darkness concealed his enormous form. He would hide in bushes, up trees, in the dark recesses of old houses and abandoned buildings. And what he saw were the reasons they were prey and he was predator.

These people were made to be butchered.

They walked carelessly about, never seeing the world for what it was. He saw weak men and childish women. But moreover, he saw WHITE men and women.

Much later, as he honed his skills to blend into any social setting, he would begin stealing home movies. He would watch weddings, recitals, and vacations while wondering *Are these people even worthy of existing?* He would watch them laugh and cry and make fools of themselves, and his hatred of their Whiteness would deepen.

And his realization of what he had to do would only become clearer.

He purchased a .38 revolver at a pawn shop; no frills, but effective. On his days off he went to the shooting range. The trigger guard was too small for his fingers, so he removed it. A man back home had mocked his fingers once. That man had a crooked nose now.

Alastor loaded the gun one chilly afternoon, put it in his jacket pocket, and went to the suburbs. White Central. No Blacks or browns to be seen. Good hunting grounds.

He had hurt people before—beat them with his fists; kicked them until they were out cold. There were bums in the run-down parts of Baton Rouge, Lafayette, Alexandria. They were like the road vermin, but bigger. Sometimes they cried; sometimes they whimpered. He enjoyed it.

But this was the true test. The proof of concept that he was the great man he'd always felt he was. Nothing at all like those hometown flunkies and his mother said.

This was his chance to prove his specialness.

The suburbs were where his prey were most at ease, off guard. He roamed the sidewalks on summer days, seeing them sitting on their porches and mowing lawns. They would wave, and he would wave back, knowing how easy it would be to walk across that flower bed and throttle them. When he smiled, he thought only of turning them from defective machines into broken bodies.

Yet they had no inkling of any threat. Oh, they were sure of the dangers on the outside. At night they would return in their cars and retreat to their houses. The suburbs were their bastion away from those others. Those Blacks.

Around midnight one Monday, a car came cruising down Brighton Street and pulled into a driveway. A man, maybe thirty, got out of the idling car and lifted the garage door. His shabby-looking suit and tired face spoke of a late night at work.

Mindless work at some pointless company that made useless things for a purposeless society.

Alastor would be doing the poor slob a favor, really.

Back in his car, the man pulled into the garage slowly. Alastor crossed the darkened street, staying alert for onlookers. He saw no one.

The man had gotten out of the car and was reaching back in for his briefcase. As he straightened up, Alastor leveled his revolver at the back of the man's skull and pulled the trigger. The muzzle flashed, and the man's scalp flipped up like a toupée.

The man slumped onto the car's front seat. His left eyeball had popped out of its socket and lay on a lens of the glasses Alastor now saw he'd worn.

Alastor stared back at the eyeball. A smile grew across his face, and he couldn't keep from giggling. *What an undignified way to die,* he thought, which only made him laugh more. He looked up, expecting someone in the house to have heard noise, but nothing stirred.

Alastor walked back to the driveway and looked around.

Every house on the sleepy street lay dark and silent.

He waited.

Later, Alastor thought that if someone had happened upon him, he might have confessed and said to call the police. If Providence decreed he be caught on his first attempt, so be it. He would accept his fate.

But no one came.

So he walked back the way he had come.

At an outcropping overlooking a marsh along his return route, he threw the pistol away.

That was fine for a proof of concept. But for what he had planned for the future, he needed something more brutal. More memorable.

That was the night that forged the Fulcrum.

My confession is this: I killed this man, Kenneth Allen LeMont, though I did not know his name then. He lived on Brighton Street, he was White, and he died of a single gunshot wound to the back of the head. I searched the papers. You did nothing, you found nothing. So you allowed me to be unleashed on the world.

You and Providence.

EIG_T

CALVIN COOPER PARKED in the deserted lot and looked over the baseball field where Raymond Bendall had waited for his dealer. A diligent man, he scanned the area to get his bearings, his pale blue eyes focusing on the landmarks he'd noted from his research. The edge of the Spotsylvania Courthouse Battlefield National Park lay on the other side of the path that bordered the field.

He turned the engine off and looked over the notes of his wife's talk with Bendall. Val had tried calling the lawyer they'd hired for Julian. But Kerry Conway had retired since the trial, so she'd talked to another partner.

"The bitch didn't even let me get the whole story out before cutting me off," Val told him. "You would think with all the money we blew on them, they'd at least give me fifteen minutes."

"They're looking for a payday, hon," Cal had said. "That's their job. We're empty bags to them now." He knew how much this glimmer of hope in her brother's case meant to her, but he had to be honest.

Cal had always been conflicted about the case. On one hand, he couldn't imagine Julian hurting someone, much less killing and dismembering them. Julian was a humble, shy kid who, before his arrest, had just begun to come out of his shell.

But Cal was a man of logic. Though he'd never admit it to his wife, he had his doubts about Julian's innocence. Based on the preponderance of the evidence, anyone who didn't know his brother-in-law would be convinced of Julian's guilt. In Cal's mind, that put the burden of proof on Julian's defenders. And they would need some extraordinary proof.

But Raymond Bendall's story had him thinking. Was there another feasible solution to the crime that could get Julian a retrial? If so, was it enough to prove his innocence?

Cal hoped that he and Val could find something, anything, to at least give Julian one last shot. He checked Bendall's estimate of where the mystery man had gone into the forest. Then he cross-checked it with a print copy of the map showing where Kayla's body had been found. The exact coordinates were listed, so Cal's phone GPS could lead him straight to the site.

Lucky me.

Not so lucky—it was in the middle of a forest overrun with brambles, fallen logs, and poison ivy.

Still not convinced he wasn't being led on a snipe hunt, Cal stuffed the notes in his backpack, and got out of his truck. He stretched his tall frame to shake off the stiffness from the hour-long drive, then set off down the paved trail.

A few other people were on the trail that spring morning—mostly joggers and kids on bikes, with the occasional mom pushing a stroller or folks walking dogs. When Cal's phone indicated a turn into the forest, he glanced around to make sure the coast was clear and dashed in. He advanced at a brisk jog until he descended into a draw that hid him from the trail. After that he followed his iPhone's map toward the seven-year-old crime scene.

The next mile was slow going. He could imagine someone like Bendall, strung out and paranoid, tailing a stranger and getting lost in the dark.

Cal didn't frighten easy, but the tragedy seven years prior cast a pall on the forest. The prosecution maintained that Julian had carried the girl's body all the way out there. Was it possible? Yes. But it was one part of the case that had given Cal serious pause.

Not only was Julian not a violent guy, he wasn't a strong guy. Or at least he hadn't been at the time. Even at twenty-three, he was short and skinny. He looked more like an adolescent than a man, to be honest—which Cal always tried to be.

But that had been Julian then. Now was a different story.

Julian had put on at least thirty pounds in prison. And from the looks of him, it was all muscle. Julian told Cal that aside from reading and writing, the only pastime allowed him was exercise.

No two ways about it, the kid had handled the situation well. After the shock of the first year, he'd come around to accepting reality. He was still glum sometimes. But Cal doubted he'd be any cheerier in Julian's shoes.

Of course, some might say that Julian had accepted his punishment because he was guilty.

Cal ascended a low, scrubby ridge and arrived at the approximate coordinates of the crime scene. A few rusting steel posts jutted from the slope, and a depression at the bottom of the draw had an unnatural rectangular shape.

This is where the investigators dug around the spot where they found the body.

They hadn't bothered to fill it back in. But in the years since, nature had made a good start of it. Aside from the vague rectangular dip in the ground and the fence posts, the area looked much as it had hundreds or thousands of years before.

Cal hoped to find another vague outline—one that marked where a box was buried, somewhere in this forest. And as Bendall described it, not a big box, either. He was looking for a needle in a haystack with no guarantee the needle even existed.

The programmer in Cal saw the whole situation as a series of *if* statements.

If Raymond Bendall was lying or delusional about what he saw that day …

If the police had found the box but dismissed it as insignificant or detrimental to their case against Julian …

If some fluke in the last seven years had moved or destroyed the box: an animal digging it up; a flash flood washing it away ...

Or any of countless other possibilities, it only took one to make this trek a complete waste of time.

But if Cal was lucky enough to find the box, it meant there was proof, real proof, that Julian was in a prison cell for someone else's crime.

He texted Val. "At the site. Starting my search now."

She'd be sleeping after a night shift and probably wouldn't see his message until it was time to pick the kids up from school. He'd taken part of the day off from work to come out there, and though Val had wanted to go with him, he'd convinced her it would be better if she stayed home and rested.

"I doubt I'll find anything on the first try," he'd said, "so you'll have plenty of chances to come search yourself."

Plus, if someone called in a trespassing report, only Cal would go to jail. Who would pick up the kids if Mom and Dad were both in lockup like Uncle Julian?

Jailbirds of a feather. His eight-year-old son Jake would get a kick out of that. And six-year-old Addie would sass them through the bars with her hands on her hips.

Cal smiled as he unslung his backpack. He'd brought a gridded map of the area to mark up as he searched. That would reduce the chances of going over the same ground twice. He also had a small collapsible shovel from his Eagle Scout days, kept for camping with his then-hypothetical son. But Jake was still young, and not shaping up to be the outdoors type. So maybe he'd been meant to save it for Julian's sake.

The thought of buying a metal detector had crossed Cal's mind, but he wasn't sure it would help. After all, Bendall hadn't been able to tell if the box was wood or metal.

Regardless, Cal went down to the original crime scene and hammered a wooden stake into the ground, indicating the search area's center. It would serve as a reference point for him and Val to work the map grid.

Bendall had said he could hear Reynolds' killer digging in the forest, so the mystery man couldn't have gone too far from the scene.

No more than a few hundred feet, Cal had reckoned.

So Cal oriented himself northwest by his old compass and set out from the center point toward the map's upper left quadrant. He planned to place four more stakes, one at each corner of the search area. That way, if they decided to search beyond the map, he and Val would know where to start.

He had just hammered the last stake into the northeast corner and started back to the first when he saw the placard. The rusted metal rectangle almost matched the color of the tree it was nailed to. The tree had grown around the placard, obscuring its edges with split bark.

The weathered metal was embossed with writing:

DEP
ABAJO
Y
AL OTRO LADO
K.R.

The hairs on Cal's arms and legs stood up.

_INE

THE CALL WOKE Val a couple hours before she was supposed to pick up the kids. Expecting it to be Cal, the raspy old lady's voice on the other end surprised her.

"Mrs. Bendall," Val greeted her. "Good to hear from you."

"You might change your mind when you hear what I've got to say, I'm afraid," the old woman said.

Val's stomach fluttered. "Why? What's wrong?"

✳ ✳ ✳

As Cal drove home, he thought of all the planning he and Val had done; all the procedures he'd written out for searching in ten-foot by ten-foot squares.

Man plans, and God laughs.

Cal had spoken fluent Spanish since childhood, a result of his father doing business in Latin America. Having spent much of his youth in places like Mexico City and Bogotá had ingratiated him to Val's traditional Mexican family despite being a White lapsed (at the time) Catholic.

He'd understood what the placard said the moment he saw it.

"D.E.P." was the equivalent of "R.I.P." So the placard was a kind of tombstone.

"Abajo y al otro lado" translated to "Below and on the other side."

And I suppose the "K.R." can only stand for "Kayla Reynolds."

But why in Spanish? To further implicate Julian? How had the police missed the placard? Had someone come back after the trial and placed it while Julian languished in prison? The amount of rust and tree growth suggested it had been there for some time.

A dozen more questions came to Cal as he drove. The placard, and the rusted box he'd dug up where it indicated, rattled in a garbage bag on the passenger seat.

Cal agonized over not telling the cops. But his gut told him that if he did, the box's contents would never see the light of day.

A lawyer friend of his father's, Dale "Buddy" DuCreaux, had told him once, "The police don't want justice, Cal m'boy. They want a clean desk and a file that says they got their man and that man is doing his time. The legal system's the last place the common man wants to find himself."

He and Val had seen Buddy's words in action during the trial. The cops and the prosecutors had dismissed any attempt to establish Julian's alibi. Odds were, they'd rationalize or ignore what Cal had found.

I wish Buddy was here right now.

Cal was heading south on I-95 about half an hour from Richmond when Val called him. He didn't want to discuss his findings until he could show her the whole cache, so he said, "Hey hon, did you sleep OK?"

"It sounds like you're driving." Her evasion raised alarms in his brain.

"I headed out little while ago. Next exit's Ashland. Want me to pick up something from that steak burger place you like?"

"Sure," she said flatly.

Knowing his wife well, knowing she would have asked about the search and why he wasn't currently knee deep in leaves and ivy, he asked, "What's wrong, Val?"

She let another pause linger before she said, "I got a call from Fredericksburg just a few minutes ago. Raymond Bendall is dead."

Confused, Cal said, "What? I guess I didn't know his condition was terminal, and just how sick he was."

"It's not that. The coroner ruled it an accidental overdose."

"You don't sound so sure."

"His mother said that after our meeting, Raymond fell into a deep depression. He hardly said a word for days." Val paused, then said, "Yesterday morning she went in and found him in bed, 'Lips already turning blue' as she put it."

"When's the memorial service?"

"The Bendalls aren't religious. They're having him cremated with no service."

"Should we send flowers, then?"

"I offered, but she said they're not the really the grieving type, either." She audibly fought back tears. "All we can do is pray Raymond found peace and an end to his pain."

"We can do something else," Cal said with a glance at the box, "we can prove his story true."

T_N

VAL SAT IN the foyer of her quiet house waiting for her husband. With the kids at school, only the slow ticking of her father's old clock echoed down the hall.

Tears welled in her eyes. She brushed them away, angry at the ease with which they had sprouted, and how they continued to flow. She was reminded of her tears in front of Julian, which had also caught her off guard.

I'm getting weepy in my old age, she thought with some bitterness.

Megg, one of their blue heelers, trotted over, forced her snout under Val's folded arms, and began licking her face.

"Stupid dog." Val smiled a little. "Your breath stinks. Where's your sister?"

Megg only whimpered a bit and pawed at her for a petting.

Minutes later, Val spread newspapers to contain the mess before Cal set his morbid bounty on the kitchen table. Early season baseball scores and highlights from the previous day's games lay beside the placard. The dichotomy made her shiver.

Julian would have written something like "The pleasant and mundane contrasted against the stark, violent reality of life."

"So what does it mean by 'al otro lado?'" Val asked. "The other side of what?"

"At first I tried the other side of the tree where I dug up the box," said Cal, "but all I found were rocks and dirt. I was halfway back to the car when it hit me."

Cal turned the steel plate over. The back was stamped with:

cg 4 15 20 dgbhc-h 3 15 13 13 1 14 5 7 je 4 15 20 hfyifi

"What the hell does that mean?" Val asked.

"It's a code of some kind. Could be a simple substitution crypto, or it could be ultra-complex. Whoever left it wanted it to be found, though. That's the only reason to leave a clue on the front."

"What's a substitution crypto?"

"You know those newspaper puzzles I like? Each letter represents another one—a substitute. Let's say that first 'c' is a substitute for an 'i'. What you'd do is find every other 'c' and replace it with an 'i' to start solving the code."

"OK, but what about the numbers?"

"It might use letters and numbers for the substitutions. So, a '1' could represent an 'e', a '2' could represent a 't' and so on. But the way they're grouped together tells me that's not right. I'm thinking the letters represent letters, and the numbers represent other numbers. Let me work on this for a bit. I'll focus on the letters and see if I can suss out any words."

Val shrugged. "If you wanna take the hard jobs, be my guest."

"My guess is it won't be *that* hard to decipher. Patterns like often-used letters are hints. And that dash should be a big one." Cal gave her a knowing look. "In the meantime, why don't you look through the box?"

"So, you've already had a peek?"

"Just a quick one when I got back to the car. There's not much in there, but it's easier for you to look than for me to tell you."

"Fair enough." Val stared at the box like it was a dead rattlesnake that might still have some venom. The latch had been secured with a rusty wire instead of a lock.

"Put on gloves to preserve any prints." Cal pulled out a pen and a note pad. "And could you make some coffee first? I may be at this puzzle for a while."

That studious, dead-to-the-outside-world look came over his face. She knew it well. Cal was a caring and thoughtful man, strong in mind as well as body. When he was determined to solve a problem, his Binary Man persona would surface. That state of hyper focus made him good at his job, but it frustrated Val sometimes. But she loved him even when she hated him.

She put the coffee on and found a pair of cleaning gloves.

Then she opened the box.

The flimsy lid creaked open, raining flecks of rust on the papered table. Val wondered how much longer it would have lasted buried out there in the forest.

Light fell on the rotting container's interior. Val peered in, and Julian's face stared back through bubbling plastic.

It looked much younger, much leaner, and more stoic. But she had no doubt it was her brother.

To be more precise, it was his missing driver's license.

Most of it, anyway. The face from the lower lip down, and the information block, had been cut out in a jigsaw-like pattern.

"What the heck, Cal?"

"The license?" Cal's eyes stayed on the note pad where he was scribbling. "Someone—our guy, I suppose—took it from Julian's wallet and put it in there."

"No kidding. But why?"

"As a clue, maybe. Or a taunt to the police."

"Why the police?"

"Have you asked yourself why our mystery man would leave this box behind? He wanted to get caught. And who besides law enforcement would he expect to go looking?"

"But they're not looking for him," said Val. "They don't even know he exists."

"Right. But if the guy who did this was content to *just* frame Julian, why would he leave the license behind? To frame him *more*? No, I think he wanted this stuff found. But he didn't count on someone catching him in the act, so we got to it sooner than he planned."

Val sat down to think. "The past seven years sure felt like a long time to me."

"Me too, dear. But we have to consider that our man may be dead. Maybe he meant to turn himself in years ago, but time caught up with him."

"You think it's possible?" Val asked with a skeptical huff.

Cal continued his decryption. "It's what they think happened to the Zodiac Killer."

"So do we go to the police? Or the FBI?"

Cal looked up. "We can't go to the police. Not yet, anyway. This evidence could only come from someone involved in the murder, and the only one that saw who planted it is dead."

The kitchen floor seemed to sink under Val. "It'll look like we were in on it with Julian."

"They could see it that way." Cal returned to working the cipher. "There are just a few more things in the box. Look them over, and we'll talk after …"

Sensing Binary Man's return, Val asked, "After what?"

"That's interesting," Cal muttered to himself, "this pattern of numbers occurs twice."

She let him work and laid out the box's remaining contents: a laminated partial newspaper clipping, a small gold pin engraved with Greek letters, a baggie with four or five curled hairs.

Cal was right. There's not much left.

Val fished around and came up with part of a picture, this one from the chin up to the top of the male subject's hair. It was cut in a jigsaw pattern like Julian's license. But this man was older, and black, with a mustache and a beard.

The last item was a business card with embossed lettering that read:

The Weakling

What the heck does that mean?

Hopefully Cal would have the code decrypted soon.

✳ ✳ ✳

Cal stared in triumph at his notepad; in particular the pair of comma-separated numbers that had resisted decryption for hours.

As it turned out, he had been right and wrong about the code. It was indeed a substitution cryptograph composed of letters and numbers. And contra his initial thoughts, the numbers did represent letters. But the letters stood for numbers—the code maker had switched them. Once Cal sorted that out, deciphering the message had been easy.

A bit too easy, in his estimation. Which supported his theory that the code's creator wanted it to be solved and acted upon.

Cal had seen that the number sequence "4 15 20" occurred twice. On a hunch, he'd replaced each number with the corresponding letter of the alphabet. The result read:

cg dot dgbhc-h 3 15 13 13 1 14 5 7 je dot hfyifi

Though "dot" meant nothing to him at first, he'd substituted the remaining numbers with letters in the same way, which yielded:

cg dot dgbhc-h commaneg je dot hfyifi

The combination "commaneg" seemed like nonsense, but Cal surmised it could mean "comma" and "neg". That gave him two punctuation marks: a comma and a dot, or a period. He'd known what the message was referring to then, and substituting the letters for their corresponding numbers gave him:

37 dot 47283-8 comma neg 105 dot 8625969

The dash had to be a "0" because there is no zeroth letter of the alphabet. The code maker had gotten cute.

But Cal, still a Boy Scout at heart, had recognized the message as the longitudinal and latitudinal map coordinates

37.4728308, -105.8625969.

Now all he had to do was figure out how a spot in rural Colorado was connected with his brother-in-law being framed for murder.

EL_VEN

ONE GLANCE AROUND the man's office assured Cal he'd get along with the investigator.

A framed poster over the receptionist's desk featured a caricature of Sherlock Holmes standing over the perforated body of Julius Caesar. The caption at the bottom read: "This is an obvious case of suicide, Mr. Watson. Let's go to lunch."

Several more crude yet witty posters adorned the lobby, and all bore the block lettered initials TJC. Cal didn't need to be Holmes to deduce that they stood for Ted Carrington, the man he was waiting to meet.

"Mr. Cooper?" the receptionist across the waiting room called out.

He looked her way.

She gestured to a door on her left. "Mr. Carrington will see you now."

Cal stepped through the door and into his fifth-grade classroom.

With the door closed and the shutters drawn, the only light source was an overhead projector. Its familiar hum transported Cal back to Mr. Filpe's science lectures.

"The mitochondria is the powerhouse of the cell."

But it wasn't a science slide projected on the screen. It was the logo for the Alpha Chi Omega sorority. He and Val had found the same logo on the hair pin buried in the box. Val's amateur research hadn't turned up any mention of Kayla being a member. But the professional they'd hired seemed to have his own opinion.

"Mr. Cooper," a male voice said. "I guess you know what that is?"

Cal's eyes had adjusted enough to see Carrington seated under the screen, his feet propped on the corner of his desk. *He looks like a blonde Magnum PI,* Val had joked when they saw his website photo. He had rolled his eyes at the time, but seeing the tall, mustachioed man in person, Cal had to admit there was a resemblance.

"Yes, it's the Greek letters from that sorority pin we found," he responded to Carrington's question. "So Kayla was a member?"

"That's the thing," Carrington said. "George Mason doesn't even have an Alpha Chi Omega chapter. And Kayla didn't belong to a sorority."

Cal's forehead wrinkled. "Any idea where it came from?"

"Not really. Alpha Chi Omega has over 100 chapters at colleges across America. Condoleezza Rice was a member. One of the Kardashians, too."

"Why was the pin in the box, then?"

"It's a mystery, to be sure," Carrington said.

"Well, what about the rest of the stuff—the picture? The license?"

"Let's go over it." Carrington planted his feet on the floor and rolled his office chair close enough to remove the sorority logo transparency from the projector. He replaced it with a collage of Julian's license, the partial newspaper clipping, and the unknown black man.

"The partial photo of the African-American male might or might not have come from a driver's license, like your brother-in-law's. I ran it through every known reverse image search. I also checked all publicly available local and regional government databases. No hits."

"Could we access DMV records?" Cal suspected the reply the second he asked.

Carrington smirked. "That depends. Some states grant

public access to all DMV files. Others are more stringent."

"You can't request files in bulk?"

"I could. Costs average twenty bucks a hard copy; five bucks digital. But I'd have to fill out forms with the person's name and date of birth. But if it's in Virginia it doesn't matter, because it's privileged, non-public information."

"Great," Cal muttered, "so unless we knew this guy's name and where he's from and he's not from Virginia, it's a no-go."

"Correct. And it's a shot in the dark that *he's* our mystery man."

"I don't suppose any of the stuff had fingerprints on it."

"The items were all clean. If there'd been prints, some trace would have remained, even after seven years underground. That means somebody wiped down the box and its contents before burial."

"Any good news on the newspaper article?" Cal had investigated the article himself. The clip was yellowed and brittle, but that could have been due more to conditions inside the box than age.

"A little, as a matter of fact," Carrington said. "The text itself is nondescript for the most part. It's about some gathering in what looks like a rural setting. There's no mention of the event's name or location, so I can't pinpoint it. But ..." He removed the transparency and replaced it with one of the news article's reverse side. "See anything interesting?"

Cal squinted as he tried to suss out what the investigator was getting at. But all he saw was part of a Coke ad.

Then it hit him.

"Wait, is that the New Coke logo?"

"Ring the bell, Darla. We have a winner. That places it anytime from 1985 to 1992."

"That's something, I guess. Anything else?"

"Just a bit more. You see the next ad over? Almost all of it is clipped off, but you can just make out part of another logo there."

It was pretty faint—just stripes or the edges of some lettering.

"Any guess what it is?" asked Cal.

"Could be nothing," said Carrington. "Just a generic coupon or announcement. But my hunch is it's an ad for a business. If it's local, we can pinpoint the origin. Even if it's not, back in the eighties there were fewer national and more regional chains, so it might narrow down the search."

"It's a start," said Cal. "Any chance we can get DNA from the hairs?"

"That depends on your budget and if any of the follicles are intact. But like the license, it's an issue of what information we can get and what we can compare it to."

"Right. And we don't even know who the hair belongs to. Or why it was in the box."

"All the contents seem like random clues. Aside from your brother-in-law's license, there's no clear connection to the crime. And if the hairs end up being Julian's or Kayla's, so what?"

"Yeah, that occurred to us, too," said Cal.

"And that's assuming we could get Kayla's DNA for comparison. Unless someone saved a sample, it might take an exhumation. Her family's probably not eager to open up that wound."

"I've just got a couple more questions for you, Mr. Carrington."

"Shoot, and call me Ted, for God's sake." He opened the door of the mini fridge behind him and grabbed a couple of Dr. Peppers.

Cal almost refused but ended up taking one. "First, what are your thoughts on the placard?"

Carrington popped his can with a hiss. "Can you be more specific?"

"What do you think about my coordinates?"

"Calvin, I think you're a smart guy. And your decryption makes sense. You saved me the expense of having this kid I know at UVA take a crack at it. But what you really want to ask is if I'll go to Alamosa."

"Can you give me an estimate? We're not exactly rolling in

dough, but—"

Carrington put up his hand. "Calvin, I like you. But when a client says, 'I'm not exactly rich,' I get a little leery."

"Mr. Carrington—Ted—I'm just trying to get this case moving forward."

"It wouldn't be cheap. Airfare, car rental, lodging for who knows how long, plus my rate. If you want my advice, you and your wife should go out there yourselves. Poke around and see what's hiding in Colorado. If you find anything, I'll do as much digging as you're comfortable paying me for."

I could take some time off. Or even work remotely. Val would want to come with him, so someone would have to look after the kids.

"OK," said Cal, "supposing we find something, I don't think the local cops would want to hear about it. But what about the feds?"

Carrington took a hit off his Dr. Pepper and flashed a knowing grin. "Calvin—"

"Cal, please."

"Let me ask you, Cal: Do you think this killer is a terrorist? Some sort of White supremacist—a national security threat?"

The questions caught Cal off guard.

Before he could answer, Carrington continued. "The FBI ain't what it used to be. Shit, it ain't ever been what people thought it was, but that's neither here nor there."

"Did I open a wound?"

"I was in the Bureau," said Carrington. "Just for a few years. I could tell from the jump it was full of brown-nosers: the type who liked having the title 'Special Agent' more than doing anything special. That's not to say there are no good field agents. But these days they're too busy entrapping White nationalists to bother solving murders. Shit, I bet some militias are just feds from different agencies spying on each other."

"So it would be a waste to involve them?" Cal asked.

"Right *now* it would be. You've got scattered dots but no connections, let alone a picture. You bring this stuff to them or the local cops, and they'll ignore it or think you were in on it.

Then they start looking into you and your wife. While they're at it, they might take all your clues and lock them in a box like in *Raiders of the Lost Ark*."

Cal didn't know how to take Carrington's assessment, especially of the FBI. He had read some articles about agent malfeasance over the years, but he'd chalked them up to a few bad apples.

"You must know some of the good ones. What if we go to them?"

"Look, Cal, you bring this stuff to law enforcement without a direct link to our mystery man, and they'll dismiss it as a killer's family grasping at straws. You need to give them a name; maybe a motive. I've got a buddy who's still in. He can test the waters when the time comes."

Cal smiled a little. "Your buddy's not a brown-noser?"

Ted winked. "A beige-noser at most. Any other questions?"

"I guess that's it for now."

"See Sandra up front about my tab on—" Ted snapped his fingers. "I almost forgot. You mentioned your wife is in Chicago on some kind of business trip."

"Yes, a nursing recruitment drive. Why?"

"If she's got some free time, I know some people up there she might want to talk to."

TWE_VE

VAL HAD FORGOTTEN how much she despised big cities.

Richmond was just large enough to have the conveniences of a bigger city, but it hadn't grown so much as to lose its soul. A sense of history was still palpable. Even the seedier parts had retained some inexplicable residue of the city's past.

But Chicago?

Gracias pero no, as her father would have said.

She'd grown up all over the rural Southwest—anywhere her father could find work. He'd been a ranch hand in a tiny town north of Tucson whose name she didn't remember. He'd felled timber in Colorado. He'd been a dishwasher, a cook, and a maintenance guy. But most times, he'd been a field hand, just like countless other Mexican farm workers in those parts.

Val had gone to a dozen schools between elementary, middle, and high school. *I'm like an Army Brat minus the base privileges,* she always told herself. But Val had never felt poor despite being less well off than the few friends she'd managed to make. And she had learned to love the outdoors.

She stepped into the afternoon light from a monstrous building where she and her coworkers had finished interviewing some nursing prospects. The others were going to get some dinner and watch a movie, but Val had a convention to check out.

CrimeMeet was an annual gathering of true crime fans, authors, and professional and amateur sleuths. Carrington knew some law enforcement guys and criminal justice professors who would be there. They could maybe give her some tips for what do with the evidence Cal had found.

"Remember, though," Ted had told her on the phone, "these are book-writing and speech-giving kinda guys, so don't expect too much out of them. But they know how to get people interested in cases that would otherwise be cold as Alaska."

Unfortunately, Val's interviews had run long all week. She didn't get a chance to visit the convention until today, the last day of the event. The convention was just a few blocks from her downtown hotel. With a bit of luck, at least one of the people on her list would still be there to field some of the questions he and Cal had come up with.

So there she was, walking down a sidewalk shoulder-to-shoulder with the crowd, taking in the putrid city air and wishing she was anywhere else. The trip only took a few minutes. But as she walked in the doors, Val got a feeling she was wasting her time.

And, as it happened, her money. Even though the convention was in its last few hours, it still cost almost seventy bucks to get in.

"Excellent," she hissed to herself as she dug out her billfold.

"All the booths are just through those doors down the hall," the lady at the counter said.

"Where would I find Dr. McMichael or Dr. Robinson? I believe they were doing a lecture ..." Val rummaged in her purse for a note she'd written earlier in the week. *"Born Innocent in a Guilty World."*

"Oh, I believe all the lectures were concluded this morning," the counter lady said. "All that's left is the booths. Down the hall and through the doors."

Frick, Val cussed at herself, *it might just be me and bunch of nerds.*

She walked into the main convention area. People still bustled about, but some vendors were tearing down booths, and a few were already gone. An "almost closing time so get your last drink in" vibe hung over the place.

Val found a map that showed how the different booths were situated. It reminded her of the cafeteria hierarchy from high school. The cool kids—TV presenters and internet celebs—were at the far end, near a temporary stage. The rich kids and jocks—professors and law enforcement—were in the center aisles. Both groups had tables stacked with books. A few people stood in line, waiting to get signed copies.

The last group would have been the band geeks. They'd been shoved off to either side or wherever there was room. They did seem to have the nicer booths, though; set up like little music studios with microphones, laptops, and wires everywhere.

"Excuse me," Val said to a middle-aged man at a side booth with no line. "Do you know if Doctors McMichael or Robinson are still here?"

"I'm afraid you just missed them. They had a lecture around noon that was quite good."

"*Born Innocent in a Guilty World?*" she asked with more sourness than she'd intended.

"That's the one," the man said. He had been packing the last of his books into boxes but stopped and held up one titled *Along for the Ride*. "Would you like a copy before I put it away? It's about my undergrad experience doing ride-alongs with my local sheriff's department. We discovered a body on an Indian reservation. I'll give you a discount if you promise to give me an Amazon review."

"No, thank you …" she read his name from the cover. "Mr. Edwards. I was—"

He gave her a wry smile. "I'd usually insist on *Dr.* Edwards, but I'll settle for you calling me Jameson."

"OK, Jameson. My name's Val Cooper. Do you happen to know the professors? Are you a criminologist, too?"

"Heck no, I'm a podiatrist!" he said with a hearty laugh. "I just enjoy true crime. And made-up crime. This convention lets me rub elbows with some of the big names. You know the *Dateline* guy? Met him a couple times. Plus the podcasters love to talk, like yours truly. I've thought about doing a podcast myself, but the wife said not until retirement. So, I guess I gotta look at few thousand more feet before I start my broadcasting career."

"Jameson," she interrupted, "maybe I will buy a book. But you have to introduce me around. Tell me who I should talk to about a case I'm looking into."

His eyes lit up. "For real? Are you a detective? What's the case?"

Val smiled despite her habitual wariness. "No, I'm a nurse practitioner."

She couldn't quite say why she trusted Jameson Edwards. Maybe it was because he seemed to have been cut from the same cloth as her late father-in-law Eugene, an ace salesman who'd never met a stranger. Val, only an extrovert when it was required of her, found that gift for connecting with people as admirable as it was mystifying.

"As a fellow medical professional with an interest in true crime," said Jameson, "I'd be rude to deny you. Help me with these books, and I'll show you around."

After helping Jameson stack his last box of books, Val followed him toward the front of the hall, where most of the booths were already abandoned.

"Looks like I got here a little late to meet anyone," Val said.

"Nonsense, these are just the Video People. They get the most publicity, but the real talents in true crime are the Audio People. Over here." He motioned to one side past a sign reading "Podcast Row."

Though skeptical, Val put faith in Jameson's judgment of his fellow CrimeMeet attendees. Her knowledge of true crime began and ended with *Dateline*, *Cold Case Files*, and the Lifetime Channel. Seeing the aftermath of true crime nightly in the emergency room had shown her how the sausage was made.

"Some of the bigger shows that were here earlier this week are gone," Jameson said as they strolled down the wide aisle. "That guy Payne from *Up and Gone* (or is it *Up and Vanished?*) was here. He had a real lively Q and A. They were giving out cookies, can you believe that?"

Val suppressed a groan.

"But there are still a few here that I listen to," Jameson went on. "This one here's done by a couple of gals. I think one's a Brit or an Aussie or something. Anyway, they look into missing persons in Oregon, and Seattle—pretty much the whole Pacific Northwest."

She let Edwards ramble as they walked, though Val was losing hope of finding anyone in the building who would be of any use.

"Never heard of these young'uns before." Jameson motioned to a booth near the end of Podcast Row. A banner at the back said *LGBTrue Crime* in rainbow colors.

Before he could continue, a Hispanic woman sitting cross-legged on the table snapped "'Young'uns' is a derogatory term, you know."

Not missing a beat, Edwards smiled. "No disrespect intended, Miss. I—"

"Don't call me *Miss*. My name is Yanessa."

Having gotten similar sass from more than one young nurse, Val stepped in. "Wait, how was he supposed to know your name?"

Yanessa's jaw dropped. "What?"

"You don't have a name tag on, and you didn't introduce yourself, so he had no way of knowing your name. Besides, 'Miss' is not a sign of disrespect."

"Actually, it *is* disrespectful," Yanessa said. "It implies younger people, especially younger women, are beneath him."

The other three people in the booth lined up behind Yanessa. The two other women stood with downcast eyes and flushed faces. But the skinny African-American man stared daggers at Edwards. Val regarded him coolly, and he averted his withering gaze.

"My good friend meant no disrespect," Val assured them. "He was just telling me about the different podcasts here. He's not familiar with yours, so tell me about it."

"You're not really interested," the young man said.

"That's a hell of a way to garner interest," she said with a soft chuckle. "Come on, give me the elevator pitch. Mr. Edwards here is always looking for new true crime shows to binge. Sell him on yours."

Jameson fidgeted nervously.

"Alright," Yanessa said, "but what's an elevator pitch?"

What are they teaching kids these days? "Let's say we're in an elevator, and you have to explain your show to me in the thirty seconds before the door opens. What do you say?"

The man in the next booth perked up to watch.

"Oh," said Yanessa. "We look at this true crime stuff, right? But we want to tell it from the LGBTQ community's perspective. Like violence against our community and how the police ignore it most of the time. You know, like the Andrew Telford murder?"

A bit of Cal's wisdom came to her: *Play dumb. People will reveal much more than they realize if they think they're talking to someone less informed than they are.*

"Telford?" said Val.

Yanessa and the black kid exchanged a glance.

"Andrew Telford was a gay college student," the young man said. "He was murdered in Idaho. The cops didn't want to press hate crime charges until the media shined a light on their small-town bigotry."

"He was killed just because he was gay?" Val hid her mouth with her hand. "That's horrible. Did they catch the killer?"

"Yeah, he was some drug dealer or something. Got life in prison, but without the hate crime charge, he might have been paroled some day." The young man's female counterparts nodded along as he spoke.

Val had come across Andrew Telford's story while researching other cases for Julian's appeal. He'd been shot and dumped in a ditch five miles outside Twin Falls, Idaho. The gay man's murder had sparked a media firestorm over rampant homophobia in rural America. Then it turned out Telford was a drug addict and dealer who'd been stealing from his supplier. The court had still tacked a hate crime charge onto the guy's life sentence.

"Wow," said Val. "Did the drug dealer know Telford?"

"I don't think so," Yanessa said. "He just saw Andrew walking out near campus and, like, assaulted him. Then he took his body and dumped it somewhere. Really sad."

Val nodded with them. "So you guys do other cases like that?"

"Yeah," said the black kid, "we avoid stuff like Missing White Woman Syndrome."

Val opened her mouth to ask if she'd heard the young man right, but Jameson jumped in. "What's that, now?"

"You never heard of Missing White Woman Syndrome?" the young man scoffed. "It's the way White girls who go missing take all the coverage from POCs."

"None of the victims we've covered have been White," Yanessa said with pride.

"I know what you mean," Val told the three girls, two of whom were White. "In the ER where I work, I always treat Hispanic patients first. Gotta represent my *raza,* you know?"

The four podcasters' faces soured, and one of the girls walked away.

Yanessa's mouth opened and closed like a fish's, but no sound came out until she mumbled, "We can't talk to you anymore." She and her friends scurried away like Pharisees shunning lepers.

"Jeez, Val. You could've just let me apologize," Jameson said when they were out of earshot.

"There was nothing to apologize for, Mr. Edwards," said Val. "You were more than polite, but they insisted on being offended. If not you, it would have been someone else."

"You're not wrong," said the man sitting at the next booth. A banner behind him read *Nothing Hides Forever*.

"That wasn't the first conversation you overheard," Val stated.

"I learned to tune them out on the first day," the eavesdropper said. "Noise-canceling headphones work wonders." The guy was about Val's age, on the shorter side, wearing black-framed specs with magnifying glass lenses and a nice suit. He had a radio voice that belied his stature.

"Val," said Jameson, "this is Denis Lay. Denis; Val Cooper."

"Hello, Denis," said Val. "Happy to meet you."

"Glad to be met, Ms. Cooper." Denis dropped his eyes to the floor, as if unused to public conversation.

"Val," said Jameson, "Denis' podcast is super interesting. You might enjoy it."

"No offense, but crime isn't my cup of tea. I deal with the aftermath all day as it is."

"Working in the ER, it's no wonder," Denis said. "It is a wonder you happened upon our gathering. Just curious, perhaps?"

Denis' resemblance to her bookish male friends from school coaxed a smile from Val's lips.

"Val is looking into a case, Denis," said Jameson. "A *real-world* case. I'm not sure if you'd be interested. She hasn't told me much about it, except she was looking for those professors from this morning's lecture."

"Do you know the professors?" Denis asked Val. "Dr. McMichael was especially good, I thought. He spoke about some death penalty cases that had been overturned and about some Innocence Project cases he was helping with."

"No," said Val, "I just know of them."

"I see," said Denis, still looking at the floor. "So, do we get to hear about this case you're looking into or not?"

Jameson leaned in closer.

"Wait," said Val, "why did Jameson say you might not be interested because it's a real-world case?"

"My podcast is a fictional true crime program." Denis sighed, though a small grin grew on his face. "Yes, I know that sounds like a contradiction in terms."

Val nodded. "Yeah, it does."

"Let me explain," said Denis. "I produce stories about fictional investigations based on real crimes and audience suggestions. My most popular download is about a Ted Bundy style killer. Only my guy lived in Alaska and went after blondes instead of brunettes."

Val held up her hand. "Wait. You make internet radio plays based on real crimes but with some of the details changed?"

Denis shrugged. "When you put it that way …"

"And they get a lot of downloads?" Val pressed him.

"Some of them do," said Denis.

Val's eyes narrowed. *Maybe coming here wasn't a total waste of time after all.*

THIR_EEN

CAL HAD TO marvel at how beautiful this part of Colorado was.

"I'm pissed that I'm not there with you," Val joked over the phone. "And not *just* because I want to jump your bones."

He knew how she felt. Cal had only seen his wife for a few frantic minutes when she'd gotten back from Chicago. He'd handed off the kids, gotten in a quick hug and a kiss, and then it was off to Denver. He disliked overnight consulting trips away from his wife and kids. The thought of being across the country from them was daunting.

But the view was almost worth it.

According to a brochure he'd read at breakfast, the San Luis Valley was the world's highest alpine valley. The thinness of the air had him short of breath after a moderate walk, and he hoped the mild headache he'd woken up with wouldn't last the whole trip.

Cal was staying in Alamosa, the valley's largest city. It was more like a big town with a Walmart, chain fast-food joints, and a college. He'd passed a small sign on his late-night drive in boasting of the college's many cross-country national championships.

Train high, compete low.

The day had dawned cold. And though Cal wanted to get to the spot first thing, the ground was likely still frozen. So he decided to wait until it warmed up a bit. In the meantime, he spot checked the equipment he had brought with him.

Cal had bought a small metal detector a few weeks back. He'd taken his son and daughter to Virginia Beach while Val was away to get the hang of it. The functions were easy to learn, and he had found a small necklace under a foot of sand that Addie had called dibs on. He smiled to think she hadn't taken it off since.

The metal detector checked out, so Cal laid out the box of vinyl gloves and the blanket he'd brought. He was expecting to dig up a box like he'd found in Virginia, and he wanted to make sure he didn't get any fingerprints on it.

Next, Cal pulled out a small self-defense baton he'd purchased in Pueblo on his way down to Alamosa the night before. The area where he'd be digging was near a park that had seen a spike in violent incidents, most involving homeless men. Cal was pretty sure he could handle himself, but knew that fighting should be a last resort. Discretion was the better part of valor, after all, but he would be prepared if discretion wasn't an option.

Cal repacked all the items into a duffel bag, threw it in his rental car, and drove to the Walmart for a pick and shovel. Then he headed to Cole Park at the east end of Alamosa. He got there around ten and parked near the public library. According to Google Maps, the site was in a small triangular wood next to the running path circling the park.

It was the middle of the week, so most people were at work or in school. Some homeless men had congregated outside the library, sleeping or milling about. There were only a few people in the park itself—some joggers and moms with small kids. *Déjà vu of Spotsylvania...*

Cal got out, shouldered his gear, and headed across the lot. A skate park had been built near the woods, and an older Hispanic gentleman leaned against the fence. He looked harmless, but Cal made a note of him.

Getting a GPS coordinate from his phone showed Cal he was within a few feet of the dig site. So he set the bag and tools down. After a last look to make sure he was alone, he pulled an orange high visibility vest from the bag and put it on.

Cal had seen enough social experiments to know that looking like you belonged there could get you into otherwise restricted areas. He was hoping the vest would do for him what carrying clipboards or ladders did for others. With a little luck, any passersby would assume he worked for the city and go about their business. Hopefully he'd find whatever was out there and be on his way in a few minutes.

Upon reaching the exact coordinates from the placard, Cal broke out the metal detector and skimmed the ground in passive mode. After a couple of minutes with no luck, he set it to "active". This mode would detect metals like aluminum and brass as opposed to silver and gold, but it could also be set off by common minerals.

Cal didn't have long to wait before the detector's indicator spiked. He went over the area several times, getting a feeling for the boundaries of the buried object. A brief memory of digging up the box in Virginia flashed in his mind. He hoped he'd find more substantial evidence buried here.

He outlined the area with the pointy end of the pick. Then he turned up the ground around that area so as not to damage the target of his search. With a six-inch-wide trench dug around the perimeter he'd traced, he began shoveling away dirt and rocks, taking care as he moved toward the center.

When he was ten minutes in and a foot down, the shovel's tip hit something hard. Cal feared he'd glanced the corner of his prize, so he put the shovel aside and dug in the broken-up earth by hand.

He had just cleared off a portion of what appeared to be a box, though wrapped in some sort of flimsy material, when footsteps approached from behind him. Tension jolted up Cal's spine, but he stayed crouched down, leaving one hand on the ground as if still working. The other hand, concealed from the oncoming stranger by his body, unsnapped the baton's leather holster. Without feigning surprise, he stood up and faced the stranger.

It was the older man he had seen leaning against the fence.

Cal felt no hostility from the older man, whose appearance and slow manner put his age around seventy. A firm believer in trusting his gut, Cal greeted the old man with a slight grin. "Hello."

"*Hola joven,*" the man responded. "Whatchu doing there?"

Cal looked again to make sure they were alone. "I'm checking some fiber optic lines for the city," he lied.

"I haven't seen you around here before. You work for the city? Get someone down here to clean up the park." The old man made a sweeping gesture behind him. "*Pinche basura* everywhere."

"Yeah, we know it's a problem." Cal fought to keep his tone even despite the growing urge to get the box out of the ground and get back to his hotel. "I'll mention it to my supervisor."

"Sometimes me and my grandkids walk around and pick some trash up. But these bums over there, they're using drugs." The old man hocked a massive wad of spit and phlegm to one side. "Needles, you know? I don't want my grandkids around that shit."

While the old man went on in heavy-accented English peppered with Spanish, Cal nodded along but crouched back down to the box. It turned out to be wrapped in several layers of aluminum foil. The outer layers still retained some of their silvery sheen, but the innermost layers were brown and flaked off as he peeled them open.

How long has this thing been here?

The container under all that foil wasn't much bigger than a shoe box. Cal lifted it out of the ground, surprised by how light it was. All in all, this box was half the size and weight of the one he'd unearthed in Virginia.

"Wow, whasthat?" The old man squatted to get a better look.

"It's a ... testing kit we buried a while back. Need to get it back to the office." Cal grabbed his garbage bag and stuffed the box inside. He secured the whole bundle in his duffel bag and started gathering up his tools.

The old man bent down and picked up the shovel. "You got

enough of a load already. Lemme carry this for you."

Cal waved him off. "Thanks, but it's my job. No need to bother you."

The old man just headed down the sidewalk the way Cal had come, using the shovel as a walking stick. "No bother. My doctor says I need—whasshe call it? Oh yeah, 'weight-bearing exercise' every day. She's a *güera* but a nice person." He winked. "And she has a nice body, too, so I don't mind going to see her."

Cal walked beside the old man, who kept on rambling, back to his rental car. He loaded everything up, said goodbye to his unexpected helper, and extended his hand. "I'm Cal, by the way."

The old man shook his hand. "Jonah Olivas. Nice to meet you Cal. If you need any more help out here, just ask. And tell your boss about that trash, OK, *joven*?"

"OK," Cal said with a smile.

※ ※ ※

When Cal got back to the hotel, he left everything else in the car and carried the duffel bag to his room. Anxiety tinged his normally calm thoughts as he pondered what could be in the box.

Once he unwrapped the aluminum foil and unlocked the simple catch clasp, he found that the small wooden container held only two items.

The first, like the box in Virginia, had a business card. This one read:

The Runner

The second was a laminated square of paper printed with a QR code:

Abraham Lopez

Another breadcrumb. Why can't any of this be easy?

The question answered itself. If the killer had made himself easy to find, he wouldn't have succeeded in framing Julian.

Which meant he and Val would have to work just as hard to clear him.

FOURT_EN

"THEY'RE GETTING READY to set an execution date, Sis," Julian said during his one allowed phone call. "I was told to expect it within six months."

Julian's call came the day Cal returned from Colorado. Val was out walking with him and the kids. Her knees weakened as her brother spoke, and Cal led her to a park bench, where he gently took the phone.

Hugging Val tight with his free arm, Cal told Julian, "Don't despair. We're pursuing every legal recourse. Plus we've hired a private eye to follow these new leads."

Val gathered her strength with a deep breath. "Let me talk to him."

"Listen," Julian preempted her, "it's OK. We knew this day was coming. I may be mad at the world, but I've made peace with it."

"*I'm* not at peace," Val snapped. "Not one damn bit. We're finding evidence, alright? We don't want to show it to the cops yet. But when we do, they'll have to let you out of there. Or at least give you an appeal."

Val wanted to say much more. And she sensed her brother wanted to do the same.

But the time wasn't right.

They had a lot to do. Letting bad news demoralize them would get them nowhere.

"I love you," she said instead.

"I love you, too." Julian hung up.

Val drew the olive wood rosary from her pocket. "Hail Mary full of grace, the Lord is with thee ..." That prayer to the Blessed Mother had always filled her with hope, lighting her way in dark times.

But now, sitting beside her husband and their children, the words rang hollow. She recited her rosary by mechanical rote without consolation.

She silently prayed that God would send an answer.

And soon.

✳ ✳ ✳

Val, her husband, and the kids came back from church, where they'd all lit candles for Julian. Jake led an already drowsy Addie up to her room. She fell asleep upon hitting the pillow.

"Can I stay up and read?" Jake asked.

So much like his father, Val thought with a swell of gratitude. "Just an hour. I'll come check on you."

After getting the kids settled in, she and Cal retreated to the living room couch. The two heeler sisters lay dozing between them.

"Tell me again why we can't just scan the QR code," said Val.

"Because whoever left it behind knows at least a little about websites. And one of a website's most basic functions is detecting and recording when it's visited."

"OK," she said, "and that's a problem because we want to avoid notice?"

"Right," Cal said. "And the page the code leads to might be hidden from public view—a honeypot."

She smiled. "Not the kind Pooh Bear gets his head stuck in, right?"

Cal chuckled. "In cyber security, it's an environment set up for the sole purpose of detecting intruders."

"But the intruders don't know that," Val guessed.

He nodded. "Picture a door leading to room that no one but the house's owner knows about. Only an intruder would use that door, and as soon as it's opened the owner is notified. You can dress it up like a real room, maybe put up a picture for the intruder to look at. All the while, he's being monitored; even located."

"So if we scan the code," said Val, "he'll know the box has been opened—and that someone's following his clues."

"Right. The page has likely never had a single hit; unless he left a clue somewhere else. So we need a way to see what's on that page without registering a hit."

"Can you do that?"

"Depends. If this guy is sophisticated, he may have built his site to detect any intrusions. But I'm having an InfoSec buddy piece together where the QR code is pointing to."

Val sighed. "Finally, something easy."

"Not if it's an image or anything more complex than text. That will make our lives a lot harder."

"Why is that?"

"Because it could just say 'image.jpeg,' in which case we'd have get real fancy about reconstructing the image. If there's a least some text, it may give us a clue to what else is on the page."

A wave of exhaustion primed Val to join her daughter and the dogs in Dreamland, but she asked, "What do you make of the card?"

"It looks like the first one. If 'The Weakling' meant Kayla, 'The Runner' could refer to Julian. He *was* running that day."

Val stifled a yawn. "Is this scavenger hunt some psycho's elaborate plan for telling the story of ... that day?"

"My guy said he'd call in the morning." Cal rubbed her shoulder. "It's been a tough day. Let's get some sleep."

Val gladly let him lead her to their bedroom.

✳ ✳ ✳

Some much-needed good news came in the morning.

As good as could be expected, with our luck, thought Cal.

"It's just text, Cal," Herman Espinoza said over the phone. He and Cal had been friends for over a decade. And though they hadn't worked at the same company in half that long, they stayed in in touch if only to bounce ideas off each other from time to time.

"That's great, Herm. Can you send me a transcript?"

"Yeah, but I might as well text it to you. It's six lines of, like, some poem or something,"

"Really? Is it in code?"

"No, just a few lines of text in standard HTML. The grammar is a little weird, but there's not much to it otherwise."

"Send it over, and I'll see what I can make of it," Cal decided.

"Will do," said Herm.

"One other thing."

"Yeah?"

"Is it a standalone page," asked Cal, "or part of someone's website?"

"It's a hidden page on a college site."

"You've got to be kidding. Which college?"

"Texas Tech University in Lubbock," said Herm. "I couldn't get much info without risking a hit registering. But it looks like it's in the Sociology Department's tree."

Cal gave a bitter laugh. "Just hiding there waiting for someone to scan that QR code."

"It's definitely a honeypot like you thought," Herm agreed.

"Any idea how long it's been there?"

"No, but the fact that it's a QR code means it could date from as far back as 2010—maybe a little earlier. They didn't start getting real popular until a few years after."

"Thanks for everything, H-Man. I'll hit you up with any more questions."

"Hey, I know this is like, top secret," Herm interjected before Cal could hang up, "but clue me in sometime, huh?"

"H-Man, you'll be the first guy I tell when it's safe."

"OK, C-Man,"

The two of them shared a heartfelt laugh before ending the call.

* * *

Cal and his wife stood in the dining room, hunched over a printout of Herman's text.

> year On Year, Neath The Final Score,
> in The Shadow Of An old mane,
> we Have Left In False Rock,
> bloody Names Upon Which All Walk.
> come Now, And Cease Our Pain.
> -the star-stricken, the plight Of The poor

After five minutes, Val burst out laughing.

"Did you figure it out?" Cal asked.

Still giggling, she said, "Nope. But I realized how full of himself this guy is. He murdered Kayla, he's going to get my brother killed, but what he's most proud of is this stupid poem."

"You can see the humor in anything," Cal ribbed her.

"Don't get me wrong," said Val. "I'm pissed we have to jump through this bastard's hoops. But I have to laugh, or I'll go nuts."

Cal gave her hand a quick squeeze. "Take a break, and I'll see what I can come up with."

"I don't want to take a break," Val said with some sternness. "I want to get my brother out. So you and that big brain of yours better hurry up."

"Maybe the lowercase first letter of each line is a clue. Or maybe the ABCCBA rhyme scheme. Or the coordinates are—"

"No," said Val. "I think it's the words themselves."

Cal raised an eyebrow. "How so?"

"Switch the case of each word's first letter: upper to lower and lower to upper."

"OK" Cal bent over his laptop, and his fingers flew over the keys. He angled the screen to show her:

> Year on year, neath the final score,
> In the shadow of an Old Mane,
> We have left in false rock,
> Bloody names upon which all walk.
> Come now, and cease our pain
> -The Star-stricken, The Plight of the Poor

"You know what I think?" said Val. "I think if we find out what 'Old Mane' and 'Plight of the Poor' mean, we'll solve this riddle."

"They're the only terms with initial caps that don't start a line." Cal rubbed his chin. "I think you're right. About the poem and that the author wants whoever finds it to see how clever he is."

"You think 'Old Mane' is the state of Maine?" Val asked.

"Maybe, but my hunch is that's too broad. His other clues were specific. It's a singular place—a landmark. We just need to figure out what it is and where."

Val sat in front of the laptop and opened up Google. "Plight of the Poor" was too common, so she tried searching "Old Mane" instead. It proved just as frustrating, but for the opposite reason.

Google kept asking, "Did you mean Old *Man*?"

"No," she growled, "I effin' didn't mean 'Old Man.' And why does it have to be so self-righteous?"

Cal chuckled. "Because programmers write those messages."

Val had once joined him at a tech conference. The event had been swarmed with spindly men uncomfortable in their own skins. They never made eye contact for more than a split second, and they substituted computer jargon for human conversation. She'd only made it half a day.

Val tried "Old Maine" and got several links to Old Town, Maine, a small city in the middle of that state. It seemed devoid of interest, except to fishermen and folks on road trips in need of a place to pee.

Val was scrolling through article titled "Things to do in Old Town" when Cal suggested "Maybe we can narrow the search down." He took the printout of the poem and underlined "false rock" and "all walk" before handing it to Val. "If it's not a code, these phrases might be clues to the location. So, what's a false rock?"

Val shrugged. "A fake rock, like the ones you hide a house key under? Or maybe pavement, like sidewalk? We all walk on the sidewalk. But how would that relate to the names?"

"Don't ask me, ask Google."

She typed in "Old Mane Sidewalk Names."

"Did you mean Old *Man* Sidewalk Names?" Google asked.

"Dammit, Goo—"

"Look." Cal pointed to the image search.

Among the results was what looked like a sidewalk imprinted with the date 1901. And beneath the date were names. Dozens of names. Hundreds, even. Maybe more.

"That's it," she muttered.

"It's in Maine?" Cal asked.

Val clicked the image and skimmed the linked article. "No … Arkansas!"

FIFTEE_

SENIOR WALK WAS a tradition started at the University of Arkansas in Fayetteville in 1905. That year's graduating class had their names engraved into the sidewalks in front of the University's first building, affectionately named Old Main.

The tradition caught on, and every graduating class since had their names etched into sidewalks all over campus. A litany of more than 200,000 names stretched for miles between buildings, trees, and hilly lawns.

On the flight to Fayetteville, Val just hoped the poem about Old Main and Senior Walk pointed to the bottom of the rabbit hole they'd been delving down for the last few months. She had taken an early summer vacation on short notice, using the last of her paid time off. Cal would be joining her with the kids later that day. He had to finish up some work; after all, he was the family's main earner.

Val had been planning to quit her job before the trial had drained their nest egg. Some days it was tougher to hold back the bitterness than others. Hiring lawyers for Julian's trial and appeals had almost bankrupted them. The additional costs of a private investigator, and their own amateur sleuthing, were pushing them hard into scrimp mode.

Thinking of all her family had given up made Val's stomach turn. Yet here they were again, clutching at the slim hope that something would come of another cryptic message. She released a calming breath, praying for an answer to come, and quick.

Arkansas, at least that part of it, was not at all what Val had expected. She'd been equally taken aback by the beauty of the Ozark Mountains and the amount of traffic in the urban centers. Walmart had its headquarters in the area, so in hindsight the region's explosive growth shouldn't have surprised her.

After the urban bustle, driving through acre upon acre of chicken coop-riddled farmland caught Val off guard. But by the time she'd driven out of the sticks and into Fayetteville, the area had started to grow on her. The traffic was thinner, unlike Richmond the roads weren't a patchwork of half-finished projects, and the few locals she spoke to gave her an immediate sense of Southern hospitality.

After checking into the hotel, Val drove to the campus and parked in a public deck. She walked up gently sloping Dickson Street, passing the campus bookstore and several bars and restaurants, before catching sight of the main lawn. Hundreds of trees dotted the elevated field, providing blessed shade from the hot and humid day.

Val crossed the intersection and approached the steps leading up to the lawn. A brass plate bearing the number "2015" lay embedded in the sidewalk at her feet. Beyond the date, names were etched into the sidewalk as far as she could see.

Old Main will be off to the right.

Val climbed the stairs to the lawn. As she ascended, she saw that the sidewalk split off to the right and left. Only then did the sheer enormity of Senior Walk hit her. *We've got our work cut out for us!*

She and Cal's research had turned up a few local articles. The first, from the spring of 2008, concerned the defacing of Senior Walk. Someone had noticed small pieces of sidewalk chipped away in several locations in a deliberate pattern: a star.

The included pictures revealed the star-shaped indentations to be about half an inch high with eight clean, well-defined points. One image showed a line extending from a star's top point.

Campus security had caught some students, who'd been reprimanded for damaging Senior Walk to the point that certain sections needed replacement. But Cal had been skeptical.

"Those kids they caught were using chisels and a rubber mallet to gouge the cement," he had said. *"No way they'd get lines that clean. Whoever made the mark from that first picture did it with some sort of metal punch—probably custom made. I'll bet those students were just copycats."*

The only other articles she and Cal could find mentioned that the oldest sections of Senior Walk were being replaced due to deterioration. But there'd been no further mention of star symbols.

Still, this was the best lead they had. And it fit the poem's clues.

"Star-stricken to reveal the Plight of the Poor," Val muttered to herself as she trudged toward Old Main at the center of the vast lawn. She walked with her head down, scanning for any sign of star marks.

Val passed into a shadow, but not one cast by any tree. She looked up and into the past. Many of the buildings surrounding Old Main were several times its size, sleek and modern. But the two-towered centerpiece held its own. It stood more real and solid than its showy neighbors, a stately grandfather casting critical eyes on his grandchildren.

Picking a different sidewalk, Val went on, scanning for any sign of a star amid the names at her feet.

A voice behind broke her concentration. "You lookin' for something in particular, Miss?"

Val cursed herself for being so lax. *Keep your head on a swivel, Val*, Cal would have lovingly chided her.

She rounded on a middle-aged black man with a medium build who stood about Cal's height. His face held compassion and understanding undimmed by a touch of weariness. He wore a button-up pale blue shirt with the name "Mose" stitched above a breast pocket.

"Excuse me?" she asked with an air of innocence.

"A name, or a certain year, maybe?" the man asked as he swept litter into a handled dustpan. He stood there waiting, his joyful eyes looking right through her.

"I was looking for a friend's name." As soon as Val said it, she wondered why she'd lied.

"Your friend must be mighty old if she graduated in the center walk here. This stretch is for graduating classes from the 1800s to the 1940s or so." A small smile grew on his face, creasing the sides of his eyes with crow's feet.

The friendly expression put Val more at ease.

"I feel a little silly …" Val inclined her head to his name tag. "*Mose*, is it?"

"It is indeed, Miss. Well, it's Moses, really, but folks been calling me Mose since way back. Mose Montgomery." His slight Southern accent was like lightly sweetened tea.

Trust your gut, Cal's voice echoed from her memory.

Val's gut told her to trust this man. "Nice to meet you, Mose. I'm Val Cooper. And I'm sorry I lied to you about having an alumna friend. It's not a name I'm looking for."

"It's the stars, ain't it?" said Mose. "Don't be so shocked, Miss Val. I've been walking these grounds for years. A lot of years. These grounds don't get to looking so good all by their lonesome, you know."

Val cast her gaze over the sprawling, tree-shaded lawn. "You must work hard."

Mose waved her comment off. "This job's a walk in the park. Gives me lots of time to people watch. Most folks never notice us workers, but we sure notice them. You learn to tell an engineering student from a sociologist a mile away." He chuckled to himself.

Val smiled. "I'm guessing you had me figured, too."

"Most folks just amble along with their heads in the clouds. A few glance at the names as they pass by. But on occasion you get someone taking a good hard look. And not at the names—at the margins. That's when I know I got a stargazer."

"I was that obvious?" Val said.

"Yes," he said with cordial curtness. "You walked all the way to Old Main there and never looked toward the middle of sidewalk. Just at the margins."

"Do you know where the stars are?" Val probed with some reluctance. "Or where they were? I heard they repaired them a few years ago."

"I wouldn't go so far as to say *repaired*, Miss. It woulda been too expensive to replace all those slabs, so they patched 'em up. Did a halfway decent job, but if you know what to look for, you can spot some. There's one right over here a ways."

Mose led Val down Senior Walk into the shade of a white oak tree. He pointed to the sidewalk's margin with the toe of his boot.

"There, you see?"

Val squinted. At first she saw nothing unusual. But as her eyes focused, a slight discoloration in the cement stood out. A sharp backward L was blended into the surface. It was part of an eight-pointed star like she'd seen in the newspaper reports.

Dread tightened her stomach. Mose could lead her to more stars. But not knowing how many there'd been to begin with, and depending on the quality of the repairs, finding them all could be impossible. And unless the message was short, and Cal could discern it without finding all the stars, they could search for weeks; they could waste weeks on a fruitless search.

"You look like someone just punched you in the gut," said Mose. "What's wrong?"

"Mind if we sit?" she asked. "I've been traveling all day."

"Actually, I should be getting back to my rounds, Miss Val." Mose gestured to a steel bench nearby. "Have yourself a nice sit, and enjoy the day." His cheery tone failed to hide his concern.

"You too, Mose," Val said as he turned to leave. "Thanks for showing me what to look for. My husband and kids will be here soon. I'll make introductions if we see you."

Mose paused in mid-stride. He faced her again and asked, "You're looking for more of them?"

Val took a deep breath, as she did in Confession. "I'm looking for *all* of them."

Telling a stranger more than necessary was risky. Her husband would have called this meeting pure chance; a fluke of probability. But Val believed that God had sent Raymond Bendall, Jameson Edwards, and Denis Lay to help her, so why not Mose?

The groundskeeper sat down next to her. "Mind telling me why?"

Val's last misgivings melted away. "There's an innocent man's life on the line."

Mose sat back. After a moment he straightened, slapped his denim-clad thighs, and said, "Well, let's get to it."

_IXTEEN

CAL LANDED IN Arkansas to find a series of texts from Val waiting for him. They said something about meeting a guy who worked for the university that she thought could help.

Because God had put him there to help them.

Cal rolled his eyes internally. His wife wasn't one to indulge in flights of fancy. Except where her deep Catholic roots ran. When she felt God guiding her, nothing could convince her otherwise. Not even the pranksters who'd contacted them these past few years promising proof of Julian's innocence, only to turn and hurt them, had weakened her resolve.

In other words, Cal had his doubts about this Mose Montgomery his wife had met.

Cal and his family spent the day getting to know Fayetteville. The kids' only lament was that their blue heelers, Megg and Lola, had missed out on the trails that meandered for miles through the countryside. Watching his wife chase their kids down a rural Arkansas trail made Cal's heart ache—with joy derived from theirs and sorrow at what lay ahead.

It pained him to see some of that apprehension on Val's face. The torment of waiting for answers was worse for her because Julian was always on her mind.

Every day was one less day with him.

But as Mose talked with them over pizza that night, Cal's doubts ebbed. The groundskeeper had brought along his nephew Dwayne, a sophomore at the university majoring in computer science.

Something about the way Mose carried himself told Cal his wife had judged the man well. His firm handshake and easy manner reinforced that evaluation. After quick introductions, and even some shop talk about programming between Cal and Dwayne, Mose got down to business.

"I'm gonna talk to the head of maintenance about sealing Senior Walk".

"Sealing?" Val asked.

"Like the waterproofing I put on our sidewalk and driveway every few years," Cal explained. He leaned toward Mose to be heard over the pizzeria's din. "The sealant will reveal the stars, you think?"

"Yes, sir. No doubt about that. We need to seal the concrete every other year; sometimes more frequently, depending on the weather, so all those names don't wash away."

"Really?" Addie asked in awe. Always Daddy's girl, she had been eavesdropping on Cal's discussion with Mose. Seeing all the names on Senior Walk had impressed her. And she'd begun reading them out loud, giggling at some for no clear reason.

"Well sure," Mose smiled at the young girl. "You see, Miss Addie, we get a lot of wet weather. And wind, snow, and *ice*. Why, we had an ice storm in 2009 that left some of the backwoods areas without power for months. All that weather does a number on the concrete. And concrete with sharp edges carved into it? That's just cracks and erosion waiting to happen."

Cal appreciated that Mose hadn't talked down to Addie. He and Val talked to their kids like adults, to which he attributed their higher-than-average proficiency in English, math, and even Spanish.

Mose looked back to Cal. "But the sealant dries fast, so repair patches on the stars will only be visible for few minutes. We usually have two or three crews sealing different parts of Senior Walk, so we'll need to put a stargazer with each crew."

"That sounds great, as long as you can convince the

maintenance head." Cal reached for a slice of pepperoni.

"No worries there, Cal Cooper," Mose said with a smirk. "This old man has his ways."

Cal cocked his head, "Such as?"

"Such as mentioning the handful of other stars that've showed up over the years."

Val swallowed hard to keep from choking. "There have been more?"

Mose casually grabbed another slice. "Yes, ma'am. On two separate occasions, besides that first time. The university had us fix the damage in a hurry so as not to attract undue attention. But you neglect that sidewalk for too long and who knows how easily those patches might start popping loose. If I were to mention I noticed one or two coming loose, it would seem to me the maintenance head would want the sealing done sooner rather than later."

※ ※ ※

As promised, Mose convinced the head of maintenance to start sealing the following Tuesday. Cal and Val bought overalls like the work crew's for Dwayne and themselves and small notepads to record star locations. The plan was to jot down the name and graduation year of each starred name and to snap a picture with their phones.

"Don't forget to note and photograph each star with a line extending from it," said Cal. "I have a hunch it's important."

Mose told the crews they'd have an Engineering Department intern and a couple of grad student observers tagging along. With most of the staff and administrators gone, he figured they'd be able to seal Senior Walk by Friday. That would leave a whole week before the start of summer classes, the better to avoid awkward questions.

There were three crews. Mose's took the northeast part of campus near where he and Val had first met. Dwayne followed the northwest crew, and Cal and Val took turns minding the kids and shadowing the crew starting from the south end near the business school.

Mose instructed all the crews to meet near Old Main at 7 am before each day's work. It was his way of making sure everyone showed up on time. And it ensured that no crew started without an observer to record a star patch.

The speed with which his crew worked impressed Cal. But he feared they might miss a star if the sealer dried while he recorded a different patch. His anxiety turned out to be unfounded. Cal had ample time to record each name and take a picture as the crew set up warning tape along their route.

The three-man crew they were tailing consisted of two men in their twenties and an older man with salt and pepper hair whose vocabulary seemed limited to "Hurry up!" and "Put your backs into it!" The younger men took no visible offense, suggesting to Cal they'd worked with the old-timer, whose name tag read "Randall" long enough to know he meant well.

Like most of the locals Cal had encountered, Randall and his crew were hospitable and unassuming. They didn't have the same edge that people out east had; no rush to be somewhere else, no "get to the point" style of conversation.

A few hours in, Randall asked Cal, "So what y'all hoping to learn watching us work on this sidewalk?"

Cal launched into the script he'd prepared. "Senior Walk presents a unique opportunity to observe the structural integrity of a concrete walkway over several decades—a century in some cases—exposed to the stresses of natural weathering, as well as the impact of etched lettering on—"

Randall held up a callused hand. "Whatever floats y'all boat, I guess. We're gonna take a break soon." He pointed past some steel benches to a line of shops. "There's a Starbucks over there if y'all want some coffee."

Instead of getting coffee, Cal met up with Mose. "You mentioned that after the original stars were patched in 2008, more showed up on two separate occasions. Do you remember when?"

"Can't say exactly when," Mose admitted. "First time was maybe five or so years after the original ones. The second set turned up a few years after. Ain't seen nothing since, but we've been on the lookout just the same. Whoever's doing this is a patient sumbitch."

Cal's running estimate put the number of original stars at over 100. *Why were there so many stars in 2008 and so few the last two times?*

He could only hope that finishing the job would provide the answer.

The Star List

1910	Louis Patrick
1911	Charles Quincy
1912	George Flanders
1913	Henry Irving
1914	Robert O'Shea
1915	Albert Phillips
1920	Dean S. Edwards
1921	Walter Baldwin
1922	Samuel Cooks
1923	Joseph Hunt
1924	David Ingle

1925	Harold Forrester	
1930	Hubart Arthur	
1931	Victor Ulrich	
1932	Carl Younger	
1933	Virgil Orr	
1934	Mark Phelps	
1935	Wesley Douglass	
1936	Isaac Zeller	Vernon Gellman
1940	Edward R. Carter	
1941	Donald Stephens	
1942	Carl Paulson	
1943	Roy D. Lidle	
1944	Clarence Whittles	
1945	Nathaniel Quarles	
1946	Lowell Emory	
1950	Whitney Hale	
1951	Ronald Jalen	
1952	Gerald Ubricht	

The Mousetrap Murders

1953	Kenneth Fields		
1954	Frank Ivy		
1955	Bernice Fowler		
1956	Wayne Regan	Ernest Unger	
1960	Bruce Everett	Roland Stanley	
1961	Teresa Dillon	Arnold Jacobs	
1962	Christian Voss	Frederick Goodwin	
1963	Craig LaCombe	Pauline Darringer	
1964	Randall Claytor	Joseph S. Marshall	
1965	Joel Walther	Victoria Jacobi	
1966	Noah Xander		
1970	Gerald Gilmore	Elisa Ambers	Jonathan Yale
1971	Deborah Bright	Michael Hershey	Gary L. Sawyer
1972	Nathan Young	Pamela R. Garrett	
1973	Sharon Elder	William Xaver	
1974	Kevin Rudolf	Shirley Knight	
1975	Francis Decaux	Joyce Sullivan	
1976	Terry Henly	Kelly Anderson	Doreen Yoast

1980	Alfred Williams	Randall Elmers	Darryl Elmore	
1981	Thomas A. Fulton	Cynthia Fields	Paul Stacy	
1982	Richard Toms	Ernesto Villejo	Albert Ellington	Abner Whitmer
1983	Conny Giles	Adelaida Quintana	Xiafang Ho	Micheal A. Unger
1984	Jesse Valentine	Bryan Engles	Colin Leonard	Barbara Essex
1985	Chris Tanner	Anthony Quinault	Rodney Isaacson	Alex Xenakis
1986	Shaoqing Yang	Michelle Du Toit	Alfonso Gonzalez	
1990	Ned Duke	Boothe Hale	Fernanda Aguirre	William S. Nixon
	Terrance Krueger			
1991	Scott Fenton	Jackie Simpson	Perry Flanders	Jeffery Horrent
	Sergio Jimenez	Michael Ott		
1992	Paulina Vincent	Winefred Kendric	Chance Ulmer	Gloria Nightly
	Matthew Chaback			
1993	Elizabeth Freeh	Courtney Dabney	Amanda Upshaw	Ryan O'Conner
	Gregory Redmond	Able Valdez		
1994	Thomas Quillen	Jianzhong Xin	Joshua Campbell	Erik Vifstad
	Jebediah Malleck	Karl Uhl	Jeremy Yoshida	
1995	Mark A. L. Orton	Jinlan Zheng	Chad Quinn	Jonathan Niels

The Mousetrap Murders

1996	Maria Fuentes	Vihaan Singh	Leroy Larson	
	Terrance Bannon	Edmund Ordonez	Shanice Kane	Cheng Xie
	Lawrence Treadwell			
2000	Karin Ingram	Robert Niel	Holly Simpson	Rebekah Osbourne
	Daniel L. Nelson			
2001	Tyler Bender	Ashley Munoz	Zachary Ellington	Alexis Lowe
	Allen R. James	Lauen Orr	Richard Haws	
2002	Cameron Vance	Kaitlyn Kerry	Rachel Ogawa	Marta Quinones
	Edward Tyler	Cesar Guerrero		
2003	Benjamin Rich	Stanley Umar	Edwin Wassen	Michael Hicks
	Mikael Johns			
2004	Aaron Ito	Anthony Serio	Carina Marinho	Mary Zimmer
	Daniel Ipner	Mitchell Venable		
2005	Nicholas Zahn	Christine Yamato	Diana Nettles	Royce Jones
	Adrianne Willis	Jacquiline Wu	Andrew Jarvis	Edgar Edmonds
2006	Autumn Gillis	Zihao Xi	Cole Beebe	Gregor Gunther
	Florentia Kazakos	Colton Fenster		

S_VENTEEN

THEY FINISHED SEALING Senior Walk on Friday afternoon as planned. Cal had been confident that, even if they'd missed a few, he had enough data to extract the stars' meaning. Spirits had been high, and Cal had bought pizza for Cole and the sealing crews. They'd all enjoyed a late lunch under a giant oak tree in the shadow of Old Main.

But as quickly as the first week had gone by, the next several days dragged.

A pall of weariness descended on Cal. He and Val had arranged to stay in Arkansas for up to a month, requiring her to take a leave of absence. The slow going aggravated her stress and she was noticeably on-edge.

Cal put his consulting projects on hold and dipped into their savings for food and lodging. But after a few days, Mose convinced them to stay with him in his modest home. His wife had passed away five years prior, and her old sewing room stood empty but for a small bed.

Under other circumstances, Cal would have politely declined. But Val, normally the staunch introvert, accepted Mose's offer. "He was meant to help us," she reminded him.

"Can't argue with Providence," said Cal. He and Val took the spare room while their kids crashed on couches in the living room.

While the kids helped Mose do crosswords and played with the old Matchbox cars unearthed from the hall closet, Cal and

Dwayne worked in the makeshift headquarters in the study.

"What's the total count again?" asked Dwayne, staring at the computer he'd brought from his dorm.

Cal glanced at the small whiteboard nearby. "174."

Dwayne rubbed his temples.

Cal sat back in his chair, equally as frustrated.

So he decided to changed the subject. "I forget, when did you say your first date with Jasmine is?"

The cute coed had accompanied Dwayne back from summer class earlier that week. She'd made fast friends with Val on daily walks with her and the kids. And she was taken with Dwayne in an obvious way he was too shy to notice.

The younger man looked at the floor and mumbled, "We're just friends."

"You're a likable young guy, Dwayne," said Cal. "Easygoing, earnest."

Dwayne waved off the compliment. "There are lots of guys like that."

Cal leaned toward him. "The point is, you've got a bad case of self-deprecation. Just like I had when I was younger."

Dwayne's eyes widened. "You?"

"My dad was great in many ways, but he had one failing: However hard his kids tried, they could never measure up, and he let us know it. 'Never mind the 95 percent, where did you lose the five, Calvin?' My way of coping was beating myself up about it, making myself the butt of jokes."

Dwayne shook his head. "Sounds rough."

"I was young and didn't realize the detriment I was doing to myself. Being my own worst enemy. That's why I had to rebuild my confidence in college. The first step was asking out girls."

Dwayne cracked a sheepish grin. "Did it work?"

"Ask Valentina Gutierrez," Cal said with a chuckle. "Though she's Mrs. Cooper now."

"I could never land a girl like Val, let alone Jasmine." Dwayne gave a sudden start. "No offense meant."

Cal's chuckling grew into a belly laugh. "Use your Boolean

logic, Dwayne. IF a smart, pretty girl walks you to your uncle's house every day even though you don't share any classes, THEN maybe, just maybe, she doesn't want to be 'just friends.' She has options, Dwayne, but she's choosing to spend time with you."

"Yeah, maybe," Dwayne said, "but I wouldn't know how to ask her out."

"There is no how. Just do it. Figure out the details later. Believe me, if I'd let my insecurities keep me from asking Val out, my life would have turned out way different. I doubt I'd be married with kids. It's not the end all be all, but if you can't talk to girls, your life will be sadder and harder than it needs to be."

Dwayne nodded. "OK, I'll do it. As soon as we figure out this message, I'm asking Jasmine out."

"Good," Cal said, "because she won't wait forever. And you will kick yourself if you let her walk away."

A few minutes later Val, Jasmine, and the kids came tromping in from their walk. The small house became a cacophony of conversation and laughter. Cal was glad to see Val smiling, her troubles forgotten for a little while.

Val would be glad to hear about Dwayne's decision. The other night before they'd fallen asleep she'd told Cal, "I don't care how smart you say Dwayne is. Jasmine is a keeper, and he'd better not blow his chance with her."

Cal smiled at the thought but dreaded telling her they'd made no progress on the message.

Luckily, Val gave him a reprieve, busying herself making dinner with Jasmine. "I told Mose I was going to have *Chile Colorado* and flour tortillas ready when he got back from work," she told the men over her shoulder. "Jasmine hasn't even heard of it before. But she's a good cook, so I'm sure she'll catch on fast."

"It'll go even faster if you help, Dwayne," said Jasmine.

Dwayne shared a look with Cal and got up to help in the kitchen. That left Cal alone with the mystery.

Cal suspected that the star maker was using names and

years to group his message. And they would have to be ordered properly for the message to make sense. His intuition told him the line extending from the star in the news article had something to do with that grouping.

That intuition was confirmed when they looked at years with multiple stars and realized the lines progressed clockwise from the top. Cal diagrammed them:

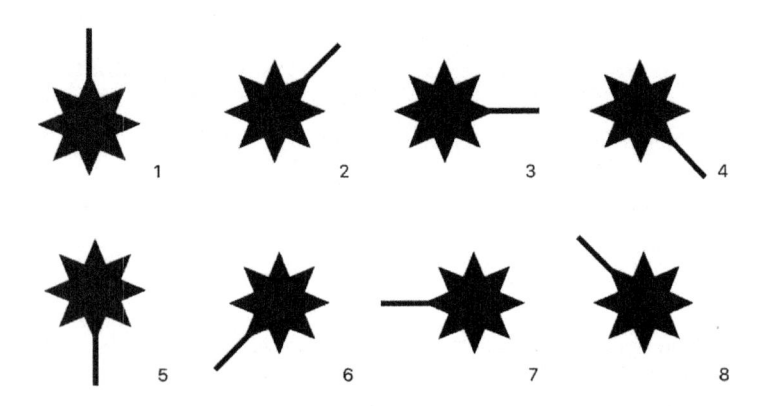

★ 1   ★ 2   ★ 3   ★ 4

★ 5   ★ 6   ★ 7   ★ 8

Missing line positions in 1992 and 2004 convinced Cal they had missed at least two stars. He hoped they'd collected enough of the others to interpret the message. Only he and Dwayne knew about the missing stars, and they'd agreed to tell Val only if it became necessary.

So far, they had recognized a few patterns but couldn't tell what they meant.

First, the years between 1910 and 1955 had one star each. Cal bet that was due to the smaller class sizes giving the message maker less room to leave his clues. The bigger the classes got, the more stars turned up, with some years having six, seven, or even eight.

Second, although Senior Walk included every graduating class since the first in 1876, no stars were found until 1910. And even though the names ran until 2018, the latest year to have a star was 2006.

Last of all, the stars seemed to be concentrated in the first half of each decade between 1910 and 2010.

But that was where the patterns stopped.

Or at least the patterns they could discern. They had gone back to Senior Walk and played connect the dots with chalk. Connecting the stars in earlier decades seemed to form letters, but that was being generous. The decades with multiple stars started looking like modern art sketches.

They had also tried finding patterns in the names themselves, or even the initials of the first and last names. But aside from a three-letter word more ascribable to dumb chance, they hadn't made any sense of the message they were so desperate to uncover.

This mystery had patterns and chaos. But Cal felt the solution was in reach. All he needed was a sliver of insight to put the pieces together.

Just how he would gain that insight was beyond him at the moment.

With a sigh, Cal looked through the study door to the busy kitchen. Val stood over the stove beside Jasmine, with whom Dwayne was already chatting more comfortably.

Cal felt guilty that their new friends were spending so much time on his and Val's family affair. They had told Mose it concerned a legal issue with Val's brother but had withheld the gruesome details. Dwayne and Jasmine only knew that Mose was helping them find a message. Despite their enthusiasm, it didn't seem right asking them to sacrifice so much on faith.

An idle glance at the printout of the poem that had brought them to Arkansas gave Cal an idea. He got up and went to the kitchen. "Hey hon," he said, motioning to Dwayne and Jasmine, "mind if I borrow these two for a second?"

"Alright," said Val, "but I need Jasmine back before I put the chili sauce in the blender."

Cal smiled despite himself and kissed his wife on the forehead. Then he started back toward the study. "Follow me, please," he told the two students.

Neither of them had seen the poem before. Besides his

friend Herman, only he and Val knew about the full text.

"OK," said Cal, "I need to swear you guys to secrecy." His joviality didn't belie his sincerity.

"I swear," Jasmine said without hesitation.

"What is it?" Dwayne asked.

"You can't ask," said Cal. "You just have to trust me and swear on your life you won't mention it to anyone. Not until we've figured this whole thing out."

"Yeah, but I can't really—" Dwayne began.

"Just say you swear, D." Jasmine said with will-breaking sweetness. "Sometimes you have to turn off the computer in your head and be a human being."

"OK, I swear," Dwayne relented.

"Alright," said Cal, "I won't go into much detail because this is a potential police matter. But me and Val and the kids are here to help her brother out of a legal jam. Solving this riddle could clear up his troubles."

"Wait, this is like a clue to a criminal case or something?" Dwayne asked. "Coolness."

"Coolness?" Jasmine gave Dwayne's arm a gentle punch. "That's lame."

The young man collected himself enough to ask, "How can we help?"

Cal taped the poem to the whiteboard. "I need you both to read this, but don't think about it too much. Just tell me your first thoughts."

"Final Score?" Dwayne read aloud. "Old Mane? That's *our* Old Main, isn't it?"

"Bloody names?" Jasmine said. "Sounds creepy."

"My dad's big into genealogy," said Dwayne. "'Blood name' is another term for someone's family name."

Dwayne was putting it together. With luck, he'd spot a clue that Cal had missed.

"'Star-stricken' means the names with the stars, right?" Dwayne reasoned. "Maybe 'bloody names' is a clue to look at the starred last names."

Maybe arranging all the starred entries by last name—

"'Final score' has to mean something else." Dwayne's statement raised the hairs on Cal's neck. He went to his computer and opened the file where he'd transcribed all the names they'd found.

Final Score, of course!

It was so simple that Cal had overlooked it the whole time. When he'd first learned to code, he'd kept falling into the trap of assuming all problems had to be complicated; their solutions at the edge of his ability. Hard experience had taught him there was often a simple, plain answer that beat the complex, more impressive-looking answer.

"Son of a bitch! I think that's it."

Cal's sudden, rare profanity stunned Dwayne and Jasmine to silence.

"Final score," he repeated. "Dang it, Cal you idjit," He opened the Excel spreadsheet that held their master list of names and dates. After creating a filter for the year, last name, first name, and middle initial, he narrowed the range down to names appearing in years ending in zero:

Year	Last	First	Middle
1910	Patrick	Louis	
1920	Edwards	Dean	S
1930	Arthur	Hubart	
1940	Carter	Edward	R
1950	Hale	Whitney	
1960	Everett	Bruce	
1960	Stanley	Roland	
1970	Gilmore	Gerald	
1970	Ambers	Elisa	
1970	Yale	Jonathan	
1980	Williams	Alfred	
1980	Elmers	Randall	
1980	Elmore	Darryl	
1990	Duke	Ned	
1990	Hale	Boothe	

1990	Aguirre	Fernanda	
1990	Nixon	William	S
1990	Krueger	Terrance	
2000	Ingram	Karin	
2000	Niel	Robert	
2000	Simpson	Holly	
2000	Osbourne	Rebekah	
2000	Nelson	Daniel	L

"Why just the ones ending in zero?" Jasmine asked.

"'Final Score,'" Dwayne blurted. "The last number, right Cal? That explains why the list-maker only starred years ending in zero through six."

"That's what I'm thinking," Cal said. "There's gotta be some pattern here. We should concentrate on the last names for now; maybe add the first and middle initial if nothing shakes loose."

Dwayne was already waking up his laptop, whose screen had gone dark. Cal turned to a fresh page in his notebook and sketched a grid.

"Peaches," Jasmine said.

"Huh?" Dwayne asked.

She pointed to the spreadsheet. "Look, the first letter of each of the last names: Patrick, Edwards, Arthur, Carter, Hale, Everett, Stanley."

Cal's jaw went slack. "'Peaches.'"

Jasmine blushed. "I make words like that to help me memorize stuff. And after that-" then she broke out giggling.

Cal looked down the line and saw why.

"'Gay Weed?'" Dwayne said, incredulous. "What's that supposed to mean?"

"Don't know," said Cal, "but 'Hankinson' sounds like another last name. Maybe 'Peaches,' 'Gay,' and 'Weed' are code words. Regardless, those aren't random letters. So we're on to something. Let's look at the last names for the years ending in one."

The names were:

Year	Last	First	Middle
1911	Quincy	Charles	
1921	Baldwin	Walter	
1931	Ulrich	Victor	
1941	Stephens	Donald	
1951	Jalen	Ronald	
1961	Dillon	Teresa	
1961	Jacobs	Arnold	
1971	Bright	Deborah	
1971	Hershey	Michael	
1971	Sawyer	Gary	L
1981	Fulton	Thomas	A
1981	Fields	Cynthia	
1981	Sorenson	Paul	
1991	Fenton	Scott	
1991	Simpson	Jackie	
1991	Flanders	Perry	
1991	Horrent	Jeffery	
1991	Jimenez	Sergio	
1991	Ott	Michael	
2001	Bender	Tyler	
2001	Munoz	Ashley	
2001	Ellington	Zachary	
2001	Lowe	Alexis	
2001	James	Allen	R
2001	Orr	Lauen	
2001	Haws	Richard	

"Q,B,U,S,J ..." Dwayne called out with audible disappointment.

"Somehow I knew it wouldn't be that easy," Cal said.

Val came into the room. "It sounded like you guys had something for a second there."

He looked up from the computer and gave her a half-smile.

"We're close, hon. Can you spare Jasmine for few more minutes?"

From around the corner Addie yelled, "It's OK Dad, *I'm* helping Momma with dinner."

"I'll manage with my little helper," Val said. "Dinner will be ready in about fifteen. Mose should be home soon," she said on her way out of the study. Anxiety underlay her playful tone. "So hurry up and solve this thing already."

Cal turned back to his helpers. "I still think the last names are the key. So what's changed?"

"Only the year," said Dwayne.

"It went from zero to one, so ..." Cal thought a moment. "Maybe the second letter in each last name?"

That string of characters, which began with "ualtai," didn't feel right to Cal. But he sensed they were close. "'Final Score' and the last names," he muttered.

"What if we shifted them by one letter?" suggested Dwayne.

"What do you mean?" asked Jasmine.

"The letters for years ending in zero weren't encoded, right? Like you said before, whoever left this message wants it found and deciphered. So if the code is on a number line, maybe the letters for the years ending in one need to be shifted up or down the alphabet by one."

Jasmine's eyes lit up. "And the twos by two, the threes by three ..."

"So for the first surname, Quincy," Dwayne went on, "the Q will be either a P or an R. What do you think, Cal?"

"It makes sense," said Cal. "Let's get to it."

They advanced the first five letters and got "RCVTK."

"Looks like it's back to the drawing board," Dwayne said.

"Not necessarily." Cal tried going back one letter and jotted down the result. He showed the others his notebook.

"P, A, T, R, I, C, I, A," Dwayne read aloud. "Patricia."

"Get your IDE up and running," Cal said to him. "Convert these letters into their ASCII values, and you can subtract any number you need."

Dwayne was already typing. "If I get to A and still have shifting to do, it should wrap around to Z, right?"

"That's what I'm thinking," said Cal.

"What are you nerds talking about?" Jasmine asked. "Isn't writing it out quicker?"

Dwayne grinned. "Bet I finish the ones before you, sorority girl."

"You're on!" Jasmine said as she wrote an E on the notepad. Before long she held it up to show the decoded message. "It's two more names: Patricia Greere and Reginald King!"

"That's what I got too," said Dwayne, declining to mention he'd finished first. He turned the screen to Cal. "How does this code look?"

```
string coded1 = "QBUSJDJBHSFFSFSFHJOBMELJOH";
string decoded1 = coded1;
int offset1 = 1;
for(int i = 0;i <coded1.size();i++){
 decoded1[i] = char(int(coded1[i]) - offset1);
   if(int(decoded1[i]) < 65){
    int temp = 65 - int(decoded1[i]);
    decoded1[i] = char(91 - temp);
   }
 }

cout << "Decoded1:" << decoded1 << endl;
```

With the output:

```
Decoded1: PATRICIAGREEREREGINALDKING
```

Cal clapped him on the shoulder. "Good, Dwayne. Now, anybody know who these two people are?"

"You think they're graduates, too?" said Jasmine. "Maybe their names are marked on Senior Walk somehow."

"Maybe, but I have a hunch these names are different. Dwayne, you should be able to automate the rest of list. I'll look into these two names."

"Will do, Cal," Dwayne said. Fingers flying over the

keyboard, Dwayne retrieved and instantiated the string of characters for the remaining years:

```
string coded2 = FCYPUVGYGTVEWVKUNCVKOQTG;
string coded3 = IHOLFLDEXGQHUFDUORVRUWHJ;
string coded4 = OIPWICMRKVELEQXCVMUYISMZIV;
string coded5 = PFDQFWJDSTQIXOZQNFSLZYNJWWJE;
string coded6 = ZGERUXHAYYDGBOKXTGXBGKF;
```

The front door creaked open. Mose tromped in to a raucous but warm greeting from the kids. Jasmine got up to join the welcoming party as Dwayne's hands flew over the keyboard.

Cal ran both names they had just discovered through Google. The top results were:

The Baton Rouge Gazette, "Co-ed Killer Reginald King to Be Sentenced Today, DA Seeks Death Penalty." (October 16, 1987).

The Louisiana Observer, "Reginald King Loses Appeal in Greere Killing, Execution Set for Next Month." (March 15, 1990).

The Louisiana Observer "Reginald King Executed for 1986 Slaying, Last Words: 'I'm Innocent, by God.'" (April 6, 1990).

A familiar story told in decades-old headlines.

Dwayne snapped his fingers. "Hey, Cal. Check this out."

In a daze, Cal turned to the laptop screen:

```
Decoded1: PATRICIAGREEREREGINALDKING
Decoded2: DAWNSTEWERTCUTISLATIMORE
Decoded3: FELICIABUDNERCARLOSORTEG
Decoded4: KELSEYINGRAHAMTYRIQUEOIVER
Decoded5: KAYLAREYNOLDSJULIANGUTIERREZ
Decoded6: TAYLORBUSSXAVIERNARVAEZ
```

"Hey Dwayne," Cal said in a near-whisper, "ask Val to come in here, then help Jasmine with dinner, will you?"

The young man got up, leaving the six pairs of names he'd found glowing in the dim room.

Val walked in a few moments later as her husband sat hunched over the desk with his head in his hands.

"Cal?" she asked with caution, "What is it?"

He rose to his feet and hugged her. Then he closed the door.

"We figured out the message," he said. "All of it."

"Then why do you look so upset?"

"There are six sets of two names. Twelve names total."

"More names? From Senior Walk?"

"There." Cal pointed to the laptop display. "Look at number five."

Seeing, but not seeing. Her eyes began to blur with hateful tears.

"What does this mean, Cal?" his wife asked, exasperated, still stunned by seeing her brother's name on the screen.

"It means this guy's done this before. It means he's killed at least six girls and gotten away with it."

The Mousetrap Manifesto - The Weakling

THE MOUSETRAP MURDERS us all.

This is a confession of the Fulcrum:

October 12, 2012

The Morsel:
He had observed her for a while.
She was the key to his perfect crime—to his next stage in destroying the maze that was this inequitable, horrid society.
Like many of them, she was a pretty little thing. And he was in full command of how she reacted to him. Because she was young and naive. And he had learned over the years that his status as instructor and his stature and strength as a man allowed him influence over women that most men never grasped. He imagined it was what being a celebrity was like.
But this was better than being a celebrity. Because he had all of the power and influence with none of the notoriety.
Not yet at least.
So he watched her and bided his time.
She was in his Intro to Criminology class, sitting up front despite being a biochem major. Thanks to the elective courses requirement, he had his pick of the litter. The class was a

known easy A that led these pretty little privileged darlings to him like lambs flocking to the wolf.

Over the years, he'd learned to sniff out the weak ones. Moreover, he had developed a talent for sniffing out the weak ones that thought they were strong.

Like Kayla.

She was driven, intelligent, well-spoken, and astute. But she didn't fool him. Not for a second. He could smell the hurt on her. She had been abused as a young girl. Later, she would tell him it was an uncle, and that her father had almost killed him.

But the uncle had done enough to pave the way.

That was why she was such a people pleaser. And people pleasers were his favorite kind of prey. They almost begged you to command them when you cornered them; would do anything to stay in your good graces.

He saw her on that first day, and something inside him shouted "Her!"

She had been chosen. So he made sure to give her the attention she was asking for, whether she knew it or not.

In years gone by, an observant professor might have noticed and taken him aside, warned of impropriety and proper boundaries. But now most academics were sniveling cowards.

He was a Force of Nature, and he laughed at such creatures. Most would never look him in the eye, and all were intimidated, not just by his size, but by his mere existence.

And so they should be, he thought.

If he'd wished, he could have risen through the ranks of academia in record time. The sickening rats that surrounded him could have been swept aside with ease.

But that was not the way of the Fulcrum. So he took care, had patience.

Universities had their purpose. But real change, country-shifting plate tectonics, needed more than simpering pseudo-Marxists in bow ties and sundresses.

So he waited outside Kayla's apartment to reel her into his net. She had seemed unsure about meeting outside the classroom. But in the end she had relented, as he'd known she would.

She craved his direction.

"Did you bring your cell phone, Ms. Reynolds?" he asked her.

She held it up.

"Good," he said.

After he had knocked her out and disabled her phone, he drove home and carried her downstairs to the basement.

He talked to her a lot over the next few days. While he talked, the people around town searched, wondering where Kayla Reynolds had gone and why.

She was frightened.

She would cry.

But in time, as he'd expected, she started talking to him; to believe he was going to let her go.

He asked her about herself, her childhood. She told him about her uncle and the shame he had brought into her life. She carried that shame with her everywhere she went. That shame drove her to do well in school, to make her father and mother forget their embarrassment and not think of her as a broken child, however much they insisted they didn't.

And he nodded and said he understood. He said he loved her.

Then he drove the knife so deep into her neck that he almost lost the handle. He stabbed her again and again, ripping at her back.

He saw flashes of his mother, of course, but that was for later.

For now, he had preparations to make.

After cleaning himself, he gathered the morsel into a plastic bag and tied it together.

He checked off a list of everything in the box.

He hosed down the basement.

He stuffed everything he would need in a big duffel bag.

When it was time, he headed out to meet the Weakling.

October 24, 2012

The Mouse:
At first, he wondered if he had picked the right one.
The mouse met all the requirements, though he would have preferred a Black.
Still, he almost felt pity for this mouse, though pity was a sensation unworthy of the Fulcrum.
Being a patient man, the Fulcrum always had contingency plans. This mouse was one of three he could have chosen. One had gone out of town unexpectedly two days before, and the other was working the night shift that week. He didn't want the morsel to start rotting, so he acted as Providence had decided.
He found this mouse, Julian Gutierrez, in the juvenile detention files. It had been expedient to his grander plans to get close to the police. They were mostly imbeciles, power hungry and crude, but they had their uses.
And they were also the gatekeepers within the Mousetrap. They let some go to places most never knew existed; even let some out if it suited their whims. But the rest had to abide by those pulling the switches, and the gatekeepers ensured those commands were obeyed.
So, the Fulcrum always kept a wary eye on the boys in blue, especially since his transformation. They would love nothing more than to catch him slipping up.
Lucky for him, he knew their childish tactics; saw through their racist snares. He could navigate their world looking like a friend, all the while laughing in their faces.
Yet he also knew that when the time came, he would need them—them and their childish investigations—to reach the right conclusions.
He drove to the baseball field and parked at the far end of the lot, where his car would be obscured from anyone driving by. And where the Weakling would not see him.
His mouse, a creature of habit, had been running of late. Every day between 5:30 and 5:45, he would leave work, drive

down here, change in the nearby bathrooms, and run for several miles around the paved path near the Civil War park.

The Fulcrum had been tempted to take the mouse while he was in the bathroom. But there was a lock on the door, and he preferred to take his prey by surprise. So instead, he took the duffel bag with the morsel and his equipment and headed to the burial site.

That done, he headed to the point along the path where he would ambush his mouse. There, where the running path narrowed for a quarter mile, the trees and shrubs encroached to allow only one person to pass at a time.

He had two towels soaking in chloroform in a plastic bag. When he saw his mouse at a distance, and ensured there was no one else nearby he hung the first towel on a branch hanging over the path. Then he hid behind a tree six feet away and waited.

Just as he intended, the mouse almost ran into the first towel, ducking his head but raising his hand to swat at the obstruction. On instinct, the mouse brought his wet hand to his nose and stopped. While he was distracted and already swaying, the Fulcrum crept behind his prey and shoved the second towel over his face.

In seconds the small man was down. The Fulcrum replaced both towels in the bag. Then he made the return trek to the burial site, carrying the frail mouse on his muscular shoulder.

After burying the box, the Fulcrum came back and ensured that the mouse's prints and DNA would be found. He then buried the morsel, carried the mouse back to the parking lot, and put him back in his car. He left the knife and other evidence in the trunk, then walked back to his own vehicle to wait.

Almost two hours passed before he saw any movement from the mouse. He waited for him to drive off before calling in the tip.

Providence again was with him. The box went unmolested; only the morsel was found.

He would go back to leave a marker. So that when he chose

to unveil himself, his true greatness would be known.

My confession is this: I killed Kayla Reynolds. I'm writing this years later while Julian Gutierrez awaits his execution by the state of Virginia. This is only possible because the racist States of America allow it. The box was there to be found. The clues were there. And instead, an innocent man will die at your hand.

And the weight shifts ever closer along the lever toward the balance of real justice.

Part III: Into The Labyrinth

When shall I see you again
Your final mask cast aside?

You who found me, beat me, and burned me
Then plunged me into the drowning tide?

I ask this every night waiting for your return
Knowing in the deep dark ground, a Monster is in his Lair.

Knowing that somewhere, in the deep, dark, ground
A Beast is waiting there.
-The Death Row Inmate

EI_HTEEN

VAL FOLLOWED CLOSE behind Julian as he walked, head down, along an echoing corridor to his fate. The muscular body he'd built up over the last several years seemed to have shriveled, leaving a small, frail husk of a man.

Worse, the defiance had gone from his eyes. It was his scared younger self that looked to his sister for answers and comfort.

She couldn't remember how she had gotten there, or what day it was. All she knew was that it was *the* day. Julian's last.

Where's the padre? she asked herself, knowing the scenario didn't make sense but helpless against a course of events that pulled her along.

Val followed Julian around a corner. In an instant she was in a room with a giant window showing the chamber into which the guards were leading Julian. They strapped him to the chair, and a bright light shone down, making Julian a seated shadow.

While Julian's room had only one chair, Val's was full of them. All sat empty, save for two which held their father and mother, both long dead.

Val knew then that she was dreaming. But the realization gave her no comfort, only dread and shame. Against her will, she walked with a syrupy gait to her parents and sat between them.

"Papá," she began.

Her father's eyes, already weeping, stilled her voice.

"Val," Julian said clear as a bird call on a peaceful summer day. "Why didn't you stop this?"

"Julian, I tried. I—" She looked back to her father. He stared back not just with sadness, but hate.

"You were supposed to protect him, Valentina," Her mother said.

"Mamá, I tried," Val pleaded, turning to her.

"No, you let your pride, your *orgullo,* lead you by the nose, and look at your brother now." She turned her back on Val.

Val's father still faced her. But he had lowered his eyes, unable to look at his disappointing daughter.

Before she could explain everything she and Cal and many others had done to free Julian, a guard stepped from the shadows and pointed to the next room.

"It's time," he said.

Time for what? she meant to ask, though could not form the words. Instead, she obeyed the guard's pointed hand and walked into Julian's death chamber. In a moment she was next to her brother, who was not only strapped down, but connected to intravenous tubing in a dozen places along both arms. The tubes snaked around his chest and face. Only his frightened eyes showed through.

All of the tubes connected at a hub: A giant syringe and plunger filled with a near-clear orange liquid.

"Val, no," Julian mumbled through the tubes over his mouth.

"Julian, I'm sorry," she sobbed as she took hold of the plunger. "I have no choice." Val pushed with all her might. The liquid flowed into the tubing, racing to the needles that pin cushioned her brother. He screamed as the liquid pumped into him. His arms straightened, then hyperextended with inhuman jerks.

Val screamed too as she pushed the plunger more, pumping more of the seemingly infinite liquid into her brother. Her helplessness reflected her inadequacy to save anyone in her life from dying.

It is my fault, she thought just before her ringing phone jolted her wide awake in a panicked sweat.

✳ ✳ ✳

"All the responsibility," Val told her husband later that day, "this whole situation—it's suffocating me."

He tried to console her about the dream. And the call. "Those weren't your parents. They were your fears wearing masks."

"My fears are coming true."

Much as Val loved her husband's way with words, she just wanted to be alone with her thoughts. To Cal's credit, he soon sensed it and fell quiet. He didn't say a word on the drive to meet with their private detective Ted Carrington.

Val eyed the large caricatures hanging on Carrington's waiting room wall. They had informed the investigator of what they'd found in Colorado and Arkansas before leaving Fayetteville two weeks ago. In the meantime, she and Cal had spent most of their free hours investigating as much as they could. *More time away from our kids,* Val thought. Though it was worth the sacrifice, she couldn't hold back the bitterness.

The main office door swung open, and Carrington's head popped out of the darkened room beyond. "Val, Cal. Sorry to keep you waiting. The secretary had a family emergency, so I've been doing the admin this week. Put me a little behind."

"We've all been there," said Cal. "No problem."

Carrington threw the door open and held it for them. "If you're ready to roll, let's get to it."

Val liked the detective's easygoing attitude and get-to-the-point manner. And Cal had called him "more than competent," which was high praise. They got up and walked into Carrington's office.

At least our money hasn't gone to waste. Maps, copies of newspaper articles, and other assorted papers took up most of the far wall. Like an FBI field office in a mob movie, the large rolling whiteboard was plastered with head shots. Names and dates were written beside each photo.

Val caught sight of Julian's mugshot next to the picture of Kayla Reynolds that had been splashed across the front pages all those years ago. She stared back at the young woman's soft eyes and crooked smile. The pearl earrings and small cross necklace were just visible at the bottom of the frame. Val shuddered to realize that most of the pictures on the whiteboard were of people long dead; murdered or executed.

Please, God, she prayed, *not Julian.*

She cast her eyes upward and beheld a timeline. Starting in 1986 and ending in 2015, Carrington had marked some dates in green and others in red, along with the last names of the victims and supposed perpetrators.

"It looks like you've been busy, Ted," said Cal.

"I had to be to keep up with you." He and Cal shook on it. Then Carrington turned from her husband and extended his hand. "Val, it's great to finally meet you."

She gripped his offered palm. "Likewise, Ted."

Carrington spread his hands to take in the whiteboard. "I know it's a lot to drink in. But your own research should have familiarized you with some of it. In the interest of thoroughness, let's start from the beginning."

A couple of chairs stood in the middle of the room. She and Cal each took a seat as the investigator began his presentation.

Carrington pointed to the first photograph: an attractive young woman with feathered blonde hair.

"On October 11, 1986 Patricia Greere vanishes from the Louisiana State Fair in Baton Rouge. Patricia was twenty-one years old, a teaching student at Louisiana State, and a former beauty pageant contestant. This last fact appears in multiple news reports on her disappearance. On October 16, an anonymous tip leads to an abandoned warehouse in the industrial district where her dismembered body is found."

Carrington indicated the photograph under Patricia's: a black man in his mid-thirties with a stubbly beard and unkempt hair.

"Two days later, Reginald King is picked up for

questioning. King is a Vietnam vet who's been living on the streets of Baton Rouge since his discharge from the Marine Corps in the 70s. No priors except a couple arrests for vagrancy. At the warehouse they find a swatch of clothing torn from his shirt and a knife with his fingerprints. He's tried for first-degree murder about a year later and executed in 1990."

Carrington moved on to the next column of pictures.

"Dawn Stewart is a twenty-year-old psychology student at the University of Arkansas in September of 1992. She's supposed to meet some friends after her shift at a local restaurant, but she never shows up. Her body, also dismembered, is discovered near Devil's Den State Park a few miles outside Fayetteville, Arkansas. Authorities credit an anonymous source with giving them the body's location."

The investigator tapped the photo to the right of Dawn Stewart's.

"Police pick up Curtis Latimore, a thirty-five-year-old truck driver from nearby Springdale, Arkansas, the next day. Dawn's blouse is found in the cab of Latimore's semi. Besides a dropped domestic violence charge, Latimore's had no brush with the law since an arrest for public intoxication and minor in consumption at nineteen. He's tried and convicted of murder in the first degree in 1993 and executed in 1997."

Despite her best attempts to put on a brave face, Val shifted uncomfortably.

"Felicia Budner is nineteen," Carrington went on. "A sociology student on the track team at Adams State College in Alamosa, Colorado. She disappears on a morning run in the fall of 1998. The next day, her body is found in an arroyo outside Alamosa—like the others: dismembered."

Val sensed a sudden connection, but the whole idea struggled to emerge from her subconscious.

"Carlos Ortega is Budner's ex-boyfriend. He's done a stint in juvie for battery but seems to get his act together in high school. He takes state in cross-country as a senior in high school and goes to Adams on a scholarship. Cops bring him in for questioning and find the murder weapon in his apartment.

He's convicted of Budner's killing in 2000 and remains on death row at the Florence, Colorado supermax. This is the only instance in which the victim and alleged perpetrator know each other."

"The Runner," Val blurted out.

Carrington turned to face her. "Yeah. The Runner. The cards our guy leaves refer to the people he frames for murder."

"I guess he didn't think much of my brother then, calling him a weakling."

Cal grasped her hand. "Val, this guy is a psychopath. He's turned murdering women and getting people executed into some twisted game. His opinion of Julian means shit."

"I'll tell the sick bastard that myself when we catch him," she said, ashamed at the tremor in her voice.

Carrington waited for Val to compose herself before getting back to business.

"In 2005, twenty-one-year-old nursing student Kelsey Ingraham goes missing over Fall Break. Friends and family think she's traveling, so they don't report her missing until the day before Thanksgiving. A week-long search ends with her body's discovery in a Texas Tech University maintenance shed. Like the others, it's been mutilated. But Kelsey is the only victim to be shot. The coroner's report lists the bullet wound as the likely cause of death.

"Tyrique Oliver, a former Army Ranger with two tours in Iraq, has been living in his car on the streets of Lubbock. Three days after they find Kelsey's body, he's picked up on an anonymous tip. Among the items found in his car is a rifle whose ballistics match the bullet pulled from Kelsey's body. Oliver's death sentence is almost overturned based on his PTSD diagnosis. But a higher court pulls another reversal, and he's executed in 2013."

Carrington stepped past the photos of Kayla and Julian.

Thank you, thought Val.

Instead, the investigator pointed to the last set of pictures on the whiteboard. "Taylor Buss, twenty-three. A chemical engineering grad student at the University of Georgia. She goes missing in October of 2015. A week later her body is found in the woods on the outskirts of Athens, in the same condition as the other victims. And again, an anonymous source leads them to a perpetrator.

"Xaviar Narvaez: a Puerto Rican transplant who's been in Georgia just over a year. He's bounced from a series of odd jobs to a groundskeeping gig at the school when Taylor's body turns up. Her bloody pants and underwear are found along with a knife in Xaviar's apartment. He has no rap sheet in the States, but his involvement in gang activity back home comes out in discovery. He is currently on Death Row at the Georgia State Prison in Jackson."

Carrington paused to let Val and Cal absorb what he'd said. Then he flipped the whiteboard over to reveal a list written in his block letters. The title reads "Similarities.":

- All murders in or near Universities/Colleges
  - All Victims were students
  - All Victims White Female Blonde Short Slim
- All Victims Killed in Similar Manner
  - All Dismembered
  - *Kelsey Ingraham was also Shot
- All "Murderers" are Male, Minorities
  - All received Death Penalty
- Each Murder occurred in the Fall
- Each Murder is 6-7 years apart
  - Except last one (Span between 2012 & 2015)

"This is all stuff we know," Carrington said, "and it can all be found online easy enough. Now for the stuff only the one who left those boxes knew about, until we did."

Val and her husband leaned forward in their chairs.

Carrington headed to the back wall, where some blown-up images were projected. "First, the items in the box Cal dug out of the woods in Spotsylvania." He motioned to a photocopy of the sorority pin. "I've confirmed that Kelsey Ingraham was a member of Alpha Chi Omega."

He moved on to a grainy picture of black man taken from the neck up. "I found this in a newspaper archive from Arkansas." Carrington pinned a transparency over the image on the wall. It was the partial picture of a black man, cut in a jigsaw pattern.

The two images were almost identical.

"Curtis Latimore," announced Carrington. "He didn't have a mustache or beard in the newspaper photo, and the enlargement process made this one a little blurry, but I'd bet my fee that's him."

Carrington stepped over to a two-page spread with a pair of logos: one for New Coke and the other for a restaurant called Har-Vee's Cajun Cookin'. "Recognize these, Cal?" he asked.

"Yeah, I was looking at the edge of that Cajun place's logo. That's got to be from the first murder. In Louisiana."

"I'm afraid it is," said Carrington. He pinned up a portion of the article that had been enlarged to make the text legible from where Val was sitting. "I searched the Baton Rouge newspaper archives. The October 10, 1986, edition had a piece about the state fair. That was the day before Patricia Greere disappeared."

Carrington pinned up a second article. The lettering was faded, but the text was identical. "This one is a color version of the clipping from the Spotsylvania box. Just to be sure, I checked the opposite page of the archived file." He put up two pages showing the New Coke logo and the left edge of the Har-Vee's logo.

"So that just leaves the hair samples," Cal said.

"Yup," said Carrington. "And DNA would match those hairs to Felicia Budner, double or nothing."

"Why her?" Val asked.

"Because the other clues are from the previous murders, and hers is the only one left," said Cal. "This psycho is tying his work together with these boxes. I'd be surprised if there weren't more near some of the earlier crime scenes."

"That's what I was thinking," Carrington said, "but at this point we can't confirm or disprove it. Which leads me to the last couple of points I need to bring up before we discuss what's next. First, the foil-wrapped box from Colorado."

Cal furled his brow. "Just the box?"

"Yeah," said Carrington, "you mentioned the inner layers were in worse shape than the outer layers. I had a lab test the aluminum. It turns out the inner layers are at least ten years older than the outer layers. Best they can tell, the outer layers are five to ten years old themselves."

"So he went back and re-wrapped the box with newer foil?" Val gathered. "Why did he wrap it to begin with?"

"Can't tell you for sure," the investigator said. "Maybe he was counting on someone using a metal detector to pinpoint the box. The way Cal here described the Alamosa site, there was way less tree growth than at the Spotsylvania scene. So nowhere to leave a plaque."

"But what's so special about that spot?" she asked. "Couldn't he have hidden it somewhere else and put a message saying where to dig?"

"You're right hon," said Cal. "He could have. But I keep thinking about what you said before. This guy wants people to know how clever he is. No, that's not quite right. He wants people to know how much of a *genius* he is."

Carrington paused to listen, cupping his chin thoughtfully.

"I've been reading about serial killers since before we figured out our guy has done this before. They're deranged, but they still have egos. And those raging egos want credit for what they've done."

"The Zodiac Killer mailed puzzles to the police," Carrington agreed. "BTK got caught because he started sending messages to the media after the cops had stopped looking."

"I think our guy is the same way," said Cal. "He wants his credit as a genius, but on his timeline."

Carrington nodded. "Aside from that, I spotted a pattern in the news articles and police reports. The weapons found on the supposed perps weren't used to dismember the victims. All the experts who went on the record said it was done with a cleaver or a hacking tool."

"OK," said Cal, "what does that mean for us?"

"It means the guy we're looking for almost always planted the weapon used to stab the victim. But never the tool used for dismemberment. Since you've read up on serial killers, Cal, you know they're big on trophies and routine."

Cal held his hands palms up. "So ..."

"So maybe our guy used the same cleaver in all these cases," said Carrington. "If he's still active, he might have it on him. And if so, it's physical evidence that ties him to the killings."

Cal nodded. "You look into that 'peaches' and 'Hankinson' thing?"

"Haven't found much on that front," admitted Carrington. "It's strange. Doesn't seem to fit the pattern of the other names you deciphered. Maybe our guy's trying to say something else. Or the words are some other kind of code."

Val sighed. "Here I was hoping a Google search would turn it up."

"Hankinson isn't exactly a popular name," said Carrington. "But common enough to make narrowing it down without more information a shot in the dark. I checked for peach farmers or distributors named Hankinson. No luck there. And as far as 'gay,' 'weed,' or 'gayweed,' that's an untamed gander hunt—at least where we're at now."

"So where *are* we at?" Val asked, dreading to tell him the news that she and Cal had gotten that morning.

"That depends on you folks," said Carrington. "Look, you two brought in a lot of great information. Anyone with an IQ over 80 could see the pattern in these killings. There are just a couple things going against you. A couple big things."

"And those would be?" asked Val.

Carrington raised his index finger. "First, these murders have already been solved. There's overwhelming evidence against every one of these men, including your brother. Despite what you see on the news, murder is a rare crime."

Val frowned. "Doesn't that last part help us?"

"Do you know what the clearance rate for murder is in the United States?" Carrington asked. "Fifty percent. That means half the time, police never even find who they *think* is responsible. So when they have a viable murder suspect, the cops are under enormous pressure to get a conviction."

Val cast pleading looks at the two men. "But if we have evidence—"

"Except we don't have evidence," said Carrington, "not really. Evidence you don't know how to use is useless. What we have are clues. Information, speculation, anecdotes."

Cal wrapped a comforting arm around her. "Sure, but any sane person who wants to sleep at night has to consider it."

"That's not how law enforcement will see it," Carrington said. "When it comes to your brother, and the other men this guy has framed, the cops have 'better' evidence. Theirs says they caught the killers, and justice will be, is being, and has been served. Coming in now with *our* evidence will shake a hornet's nest. Put yourself in their shoes. Would you want to admit helping set up an innocent man for execution?"

"What we need is a name," Cal said.

Carrington brought his hands together in a sharp clap. "Exactamundo, my friend. A name that all of *our* evidence points to, giving the police no wiggle room to say otherwise."

"That sounds great Ted," Val said, "but why do I have the feeling it won't be that simple?"

Carrington sat on the edge of his desk. "Because that's the other big thing. I'm sure you've asked yourselves who this guy is; what he does. What's his profession?"

"Yeah," said Cal, "all the murders happened near universities, and all the victims were students. We think it's probably someone involved with colleges: a teacher or administrator, maybe."

"That's a logical conclusion," said Carrington, "and you could be right. But I'd add that it's someone who knows the legal system. Policing, the courts, evidence handling, the works. I would expand my guess to someone in law enforcement, like campus security. Or even a cop. Hell, this guy could be a DA."

Val swallowed a sudden lump in her throat. "You think

so?"

"Look," said Carrington, "you get to know the legal system from the inside like I have, and you get a different sense of how it works than the average American. Most people watch *CSI* and think the police always find evidence and always put away the bad guy. They also think all cops are honorable and smart, but that's beside the point.

"The truth is, the conviction rate for the fifty percent of murder cases that ever see trial is only seventy percent. Maybe you think the police say, 'Well, we got that one wrong. Let's go find the real killer.' Nope. Murder cases are huge resource drains on the system. So it does everything in its power to get a conviction."

"What you're telling us," Val said, "is that when the cops have the evidence handed to them, they're not gonna turn down the help."

Carrington gave a sympathetic shrug. "That's what I'm saying, and whether they'll admit it or not, they quit looking for other suspects the second our guy handed them the evidence against your brother. At his trial, there were indications of foreign DNA on the rope and the knife. The police chalked it up to cross contamination. But what if it wasn't? What if it was our guy's DNA?"

Cal's eyes brightened. "Couldn't we use that foreign DNA to get our guy's name?"

Carrington shook his head. "Not unless he's a criminal who's already in the FBI's or some state's database. If they were diligent, they would have done that during the investigation just for thoroughness, but like I said, if they already had their guy, why bother? Why muddy the waters of an open and shut case?"

Val let out a long, shuddering breath. Cal sat back, his furrowed brow showing he was deep in thought. Only the buzz of florescent lights and the faint ticking of the clock over the door sullied the silence.

"So," Cal said at last, "you alluded to what's next. Not contacting the authorities, I assume?"

"Not yet," the investigator said. "I'll talk to my guy in the FBI in the vaguest terms I can to gauge how much help they might be. Don't get your hopes up, though."

"We've already touched that hot stove enough times," said Val.

Carrington gave a knowing, bitter laugh. "I'll try to find connections between these other cases. If our guy left these clues out in the open, could be he's left some online, too."

"Searching online is one of the first things we tried," said Cal. "You sound pretty sure there's more we overlooked."

"Something bugs me about him going back to Colorado and re-wrapping that box," Carrington said. "It also bugs me that he used a QR code. Like you said Cal, those things didn't get popular until 2010 or so."

Cal picked up the investigator's thread. "If the older layer of foil is twenty years old, that means the box was buried around the year 2000."

"The girl from Colorado was killed in 1998," said Carrington. "Maybe he swapped something he buried back then for the code."

"And if so," Val finished, "why?"

Carrington shot her an approving wink. "Anyway, that's my plan. If you'll approve the expense for, say, twenty more hours?"

"That sounds fine, Ted." Despite his bold words, Cal's face looked pinched.

"Was it something I said?" Carrington asked.

Val shared a look with her husband and said, "Sussex State Prison called this morning. Julian's execution date has been set."

NIN_TEEN

"VALENTINA GUTIERREZ-COOPER?" a voice echoed from the shadows to Val's left as she stepped from the hospital and into the parking deck.

Val's habit of checking the surveillance monitors before leaving work left her unsurprised to see a man standing beside a concrete column. She *was* surprised to be called by name, including her maiden name.

Projecting a calm demeanor, Val released the safety on the mace canister in her right hand. "Who's asking, please?"

A middle-aged Caucasian male stepped into the dim florescent lighting. "I'm with the FBI, ma'am."

Something about him struck Val as familiar. *He didn't identify himself, just his organization—as a diversion. Or intimidation.* "Am I supposed to take your word on that?"

The man produced a leather badge holder containing a laminated ID card with "FBI" written in large bold letters in the center. The name on the ID explained why its holder seemed familiar.

"Edward Mertz," said Val. "You were with Fredericksburg PD. Or was it the Spotsylvania Sheriff's Office?"

"I was a Spotsylvania County deputy when I caught your brother for murdering that girl," Mertz spat.

"But you didn't really catch him, did you?" Val retorted. "He was driving by the scene, and you happened to be there on an anonymous tip about the girl my brother allegedly killed. Isn't that right, Mr. Mertz?"

"*Special Agent* Mertz. And he was convicted, so there's no 'alleged' anything. He murdered and hacked up that girl."

"Right," Val said flatly. "The Bureau must have noticed your stellar police work. Congrats."

"The Bureau couldn't care less about that case," Mertz said acidly. "Let's dispense with pointless verbal sparring. It's a waste of time."

Val's icy front cracked a bit. "You were waiting for *me* in a dark parking garage. If you wanted to save time, you could've called during my twelve-hour shift. Or called me at home, I'm sure the FBI could find my number."

"Consider this an 'off-the-books' meeting," said Mertz.

"Or a warning?" Val accused him. "The FBI may not care about my brother, but I know why *you* should."

"And why is that?" Mertz asked.

"Because if you're here, it means you know you messed up."

"Wrong." Mertz stabbed a finger at Val. "It means you don't know that sticking your nose into a closed case is a great way to get charged with evidence tampering and obstructing justice. And make no mistake: You, your husband, or anyone else that keeps playing detective in the Reynolds case *will* be charged."

He doesn't know about the other cases. "And you came alone on this ultra-important mission? I'd have thought that went against protocol. Then again, having a witness might make it harder to set me up for a process crime."

"Watch your words, Ms. Cooper," said Mertz. "Both of your parents are dead, so your children would have to be placed with Child Protective Services in the event of you and your husband's arrest."

Val gripped the mace a little tighter but held her tongue. Mertz had shown his hand without knowing it. *As soon as someone injects emotion into a debate, they're treading water, drowning, and just hoping to pull you down with them.*

She inhaled slowly, and in a softened voice said, "Listen, I apologize for being rude, Special Agent Mertz. I had a crazy night at work. And I'm not sure if you're in the loop about this yet, but my brother's execution date has been set. Guess I'm a little moody."

Mertz's posture relaxed slightly. "You admit that you've been looking into the Reynolds case, then?"

"Agent Mertz, my brother doesn't have much time left. Not time for another appeal, and he'll likely not even be considered for a commuted sentence. I know he's probably gonna die, and soon."

Val looked down, and in that moment a memory came to her.

Julian was six, she about nine or ten, and they were still in Colorado, her parents still alive. Her father let them go downstream a ways, telling Val to help Julian cast with his new pole. Julian with his always-mussed hair, wanting to chase grasshoppers or draw in the dirt rather than fish. But Papá had told him to catch fish, and had bought the pole for him, so there he was. Never intending to catch anything, when the trout got hooked little Julian was horrified. Val brought it in and was ready to put it in her creel when Julian pleaded with her to stop. From upstream Papá was shouting Una trucha, mijitos? Val looking at her brother, then crouching down and let the rainbow slip away into the stream again. No, Papá, he got away. Julian wrapping his arms around her, burying his face into her side.

Her eyes welled, and when she looked back up her lids were overwhelmed with tears. "But what kind of sister would I be if I didn't try to help him anyway?"

Mertz's scowl vanished. He produced a business card from his wallet. "Just tell that PI you hired to contact me directly if he has any more questions. We don't need him skulking around riling people up unnecessarily."

Val took his card. "I understand." She wiped her eyes with the back of her hand. "Could I get another card? I'd like one to keep, just in case something comes up."

He paused for a moment but handed her a second card.

Mertz walked Val to her car, she put on the mousiest

persona she could stomach and even waved to him as she backed up.

"Fucking schmuck," she whispered to herself as she drove away.

* * *

In a rare lapse of emotional control, Cal fumed when Val told him about Mertz, specifically the Agent's veiled threat of putting their kids with Child Protective Services. "We payed through the nose for a lawyer once. What's one more? I should haul his ass into court for harassment!"

For once, Val played the voice of reason. "Mertz was grasping at air. He built his career on Kayla Reynolds, so any suggestion he botched that case would kill his reputation."

The living room phone rang. Neither Cal nor his wife recognized the number. But when it went to voicemail, it was Ted Carrington.

"I owe you an apology, Cal," the investigator said when they called him back. "There may be one good apple left in the FBI barrel, but it's not anyone I know. Not anymore."

"Sorry to hear it. Where are you calling from, Ted?"

"My office might be compromised," Carrington warned. "This is a burner. Let's meet at your house, just as a precaution."

Cal strode to the window and closed the curtains. "What if they're staking us out?"

"I doubt it. From what Val said, that little meet and greet was a scare tactic. A probe to see if we gave up information they didn't want getting out."

"What time works for you?" asked Cal.

"How about right now? I thought you'd be game, so I took the liberty of heading over."

Cal gestured to the front door. Val opened it, and after recovering from a brief start, she ushered Carrington inside.

"So," Cal asked the investigator. "To what do we owe the pleasure?"

"I had a less-than-cordial visit from a man called Mertz. Name sound familiar?" asked Carrington.

Cal maintained his calm yet couldn't help balling his fists.

"That SOB made a traffic stop," said Val. "Now he's spun it into solving a murder single-handed."

"You're right about 'a murder,'" said Carrington. "Mertz only asked me about the Reynolds case. He gave no indication the FBI knows of any connection to the other killings. But seeing how rustled his jimmies are, I'm guessing he's privy to evidence that didn't come out in court. And he wants to make sure it never sees the light of day."

"Evidence that would have damaged the prosecution's case?" Cal said.

"Going off Raymond Bendall's description of the burial site," said Carrington, "there must have been evidence someone else was there. If it got out that police ignored evidence of another suspect, it would set off a firestorm against the local cops and the feds."

"And it would strengthen Julian's case on appeal," Cal added.

"So what does that mean for us?" Val asked.

"It means you two and your kids should get out of town ASAP. Might I suggest Columbia, Missouri?"

Cal recovered from the shock first. "Why Missouri?"

"You found something, didn't you," said Val. "A lead."

A small grin grew on Carrington's face. He sat on the couch and opened his laptop on the coffee table. "I was gonna tell you all about this earlier, until the FBI came calling. It occurred to me the bastards just might come back with a warrant."

"And find all the evidence we've gathered," said Cal.

Val clutched his arm. "Then what?"

Carrington shrugged. "Who knows? They might find this guy for us. The FBI likes to think they're the elite of the law enforcement elite. But at the end of the day, they're just cops. And cops hate investigating crimes they've already solved."

"What are you saying?" Cal asked.

"I'm saying you're my clients. And if you want me to hand

everything over to the feds, just say the word."

"Screw that," said Val.

"Good," Carrington said. "Now, don't get your hopes up. This could be one more step that leads to another step. But somehow I don't think so."

He opened Facebook, pulled a small notepad from his jacket pocket, and flipped to a page scrawled with notes.

"When we last met," said Carrington, "I'd exhausted all our evidence about the victims and alleged perpetrators. But I kept thinking about how our guy left all those names out in the open. And about that QR code leading to a website. It's accessible, you just have to know how to get there. So I got on social media to look for connections with the names we had."

"And you turned up something our web searches missed?" Cal inferred.

Carrington motioned for patience. "Now there are *a lot* of true crime pages on Facebook. But the bulk of them are for unsolved cases. Most of the rest are memorials set up by victims' families, and those are more recent, as in since Facebook was a thing."

Cal watched as the investigator opened several Facebook tabs.

"So I searched for pages in our victims' names," said Carrington, "starting with the most recent, Taylor Buss. Her family set up a missing person page in 2015. When her body was found, they turned it into a memorial page."

Scanning the page, Cal saw it had about a hundred followers, posts from Taylor's friends and family, and annual updates for a candlelight vigil on her birthday.

Carrington switched tabs. "But there's also this other one: same setup, with pictures and articles from when she went missing and from the trial. But it was made about a year after she was murdered and has zero followers."

"Because it's a private page," Cal noted.

"Exactly," said Carrington. "And it only has one administrator named Tace X. McKinna."

"That's a strange name," Val said.

"Sounds made up. But also familiar somehow," Cal mentioned.

"Right," Carrington continued. "I looked it up but couldn't find one instance in any database. But it gets better. Kayla's family also set up a Facebook page up in 2012. Same pattern; couple hundred followers, bunch of comments early on with pictures and posts about the trial. And again, there's another page; private, little activity, started a year after her death. With a single administrator."

"Same name?" Cal asked.

"Close enough to catch my interest," said Carrington. "Dayes Hecks-MacKenna. It's not in any database either, so it —"

"Son of a bitch," Cal hissed.

Val and Carrington both stared.

"Sorry," said Cal, "but you saying those names out loud makes it obvious they're pseudonyms for *deus ex machina*. You know, when the author of a story bails out a stuck character by unconventional means?"

"Sounds like cheating," Val said.

Cal grinned. "Sounds like our guy is tipping his hand."

"But," Carrington said, "no one else knows these murders are connected. You can't see the similarities until you see the whole picture. Which you can't see on Facebook, since some of the murders predate it."

"What about the other ones that do predate it?" asked Cal.

"I thought you'd never ask," said Carrington. "Kelsey Ingraham, Felicia Budner, Dawn Stewart, and Patricia Greere all have pages created in 2010 by admins using variations of that same name. I even tracked down a post by Felicia Budner's sister, upset that someone unconnected to the family made her a memorial page."

"How much you wanna bet all those admins are the same guy?" Val said.

"Oh, five times what you're paying me," said Carrington. "Since he also left these ..." He scrolled down to several newspaper pictures of Patricia Greere and stopped on an image that was out of place among the beauty pageant and high school yearbook photos. Out-of-focus, dark, and almost solid red, it had metallic lines at the bottom edge.

Val squinted. "What is that? Looks like someone snapped a picture by accident."

"Cal?" the investigator asked.

"I'd guess it's part of a bigger image."

Carrington switched to Dawn Stewart's Facebook page and clicked on another image like the last one. "All the *deus ex machina* pages have one like this."

Though blurry, Cal made out the letters 'Ca' and part of another. "It's a word, but I can't tell what it is."

"Let me spare you the suspense." Carrington opened a file of the six images pasted together. Two pictures seemed to be missing, but it was obviously a book cover.

"*Cauldron of* ... something," Cal read.

"Now let me save you some time." Carrington opened a clear image of the whole cover.

"*Cauldron of Empires* by N.R. Dahlgren," said Val. "Is that our guy?"

"No," said Carrington, "it's not our guy. Nor is there much history on him. Dahlgren was big into the 1920s Progressive movement. Later, he started some kind of cult and died in the early 1960s."

"No exact date?" Cal asked.

Carrington chuckled. "Authorities aren't even sure about the status and location of his body. His followers just announced he was gone, and the group disbanded a few years later."

"What about the book itself?" asked Val.

The investigator shrugged. "It's about empires and revolutions, or Dahlgren's take on them, anyway; predicts a race war in America."

"Did you track down a copy?" asked Cal.

"It had a limited pressing in the 1950s with a small California publisher," said Carrington. "There's just scattered excerpts online. And let me tell you, the little I found is some weird stuff.

Cal pointed to the screen. "Go back to those pictures—the six cover pieces from Facebook."

Carrington clicked on the file, bringing it to the forefront.

"They're not out of focus, are they?" Cal said. "They've been digitally modified."

He and Carrington shared a look.

"OK wise guys," said Val, "what's the big deal with them being modified?"

"Steganography," Cal said.

The private investigator nodded.

Val's brow furled. "Like Jake's toy dinosaur?"

"Steganography is hiding a message within a file," said Cal. "Doing this digitally means messing with the 0s and 1s to hide a secret, but when you do that to digital photos it messes with the clarity of the original picture."

"Great," Val sighed. "More messages. What's our guy saying with this one?"

"In this case, it's two," said Carrington. "He's letting us know this book is important. He is also hiding a message in the pictures themselves."

"How do you decipher it?" Val asked.

"You run decoding software," said Cal, "which I'm guessing Ted's already had one of his tech guys do."

Carrington smiled. "You know me too well."

"So what did you find?" Cal asked.

"Addresses," Carrington said.

"Addresses?" the Coopers said at the same time.

Carrington showed his palms in a placating gesture. "Relax, if I had the killer's address, I'd have called you right away. No, the pictures from the pre-Facebook era pages all contained the address of a library at George Mason University."

"George Mason?" Val said. "That's where Kayla went."

"And the picture from Kayla's page has the address for the library at University of Georgia. Which is where Taylor Buss was a student."

"So if the pattern holds," Cal said, "the picture from

Taylor's page identifies the school our guy's next victim is attending."

"The University of Missouri in Columbia," said Carrington. "Where I'd bet there's a copy of Dahlgren's book just waiting to be found."

Val flashed a grin at the PI. "I knew you didn't suggest Missouri for the scenery."

"What about George Mason and the University of Georgia?" Cal asked.

"Agent Mertz interrupted before I could call them," said Carrington. "But my gut says this guy takes his copy with him when he moves."

Cal focused his intense gaze on the investigator. "Ted, get on the horn with the library in Missouri, and see if by chance they have a record of this book. I doubt it'll be that easy, but it's worth a shot. I'll head up to Fairfax tomorrow and check at George Mason, just in case."

"Denis has been breathing down my neck since his episode based on Julian's case blew up," said Val. "We need to decide how much of this new stuff to let him in on."

"Julian has less than three months left," said Cal. "Whatever we find, when we get back from Missouri, we go the police and let the chips fall where they may."

"Good thinking," said Carrington.

Everyone stood, and the Coopers shook hands with Carrington. On his way out, the investigator paused at the door. "I almost forgot. Besides the addresses, the pictures all had one message in common. It doesn't make any sense to me right now, but maybe when we find that book it'll clue us in."

The message read:

"a king must be unafraid of Burning Jesters in order to keep his kingdom."

TWEN_Y

CAL SPENT A full day scouring George Mason's four libraries with no luck. And Carrington called the University of Missouri library and confirmed that *Cauldron of Empires* wasn't in their catalog.

Which lent more weight to Carrington's theory that the killer traveled with one copy of the book—and that their best hope of finding it lay in Missouri.

Taking another leave of absence from work was little more than an afterthought to Val. But leaving the kids with friends gave her pause.

"Me and Jake went with you to Arkansas," Addie had complained. "Why can't we come with you to Missouri?"

"If we get stuck and need help," Cal had told their daughter, "I'll fly you out there with us. OK, little bird?"

"Promise?" Addie had said more than asked.

"Promise." Cal and Addie had shaken on it. And he'd told Jake to look after her.

But on the car ride out, Val got the haunting notion that she would never see her children again.

❋ ❋ ❋

May Christ guide us swiftly to this book, Val prayed as she and Cal entered Elmer Ellis Library at the University of Missouri. The large arched windows gave the impression of a cathedral.

Only the stained-glass visages of Christ and the saints were missing.

The musty yet inviting smell of old books hit Val's nose. She'd always appreciated old libraries and small bookstores. The odor of thousands, maybe millions, of pages added to the sense of history that slick big box bookstores with attached coffee bars lacked.

"They're the fast food joints of literature," Cal had said when they were still dating.

Maybe that was when I first fell in love with him, Val thought as her husband studied the library's layout on a kiosk map.

Despite their best-laid plans, it all came down to guesswork. Every clue contained another puzzle, an exercise in decrypting a madman's ego. But Val felt that they were close now; so close that she cast reflexive glances at the library's other patrons, wondering if any could be the one.

She remembered Raymond Bendall's description: tall; and strong enough to carry Julian, who'd weighed 130 pounds, like it was nothing. Such a man was capable of cruelty she could scarcely fathom.

They were chasing a monster.

No, hunting *one.*

She and Cal searched the stacks for hours, looking for the telltale cover, title, and author name.

"I don't want to give our guy more credit than he deserves," Cal said, "but a library is the best place to hide a book."

"We could find any other one in this whole place instantly with a catalog search," Val said as she ran her finger along a row of labeled spines.

"That's the point of leaving it unregistered. We have to figure out where our guy left it."

"And we need to figure out what 'Burning Jesters' means," Val reminded him. The term had been on her mind since Carrington had shown it to them. It reminded her of the poem that had led them to Senior Walk. Capitalizing those two words highlighted their significance.

"Yeah," said Cal, "It bugs me. Not just that I can't decipher what it means. Why is that same phrase hidden in all six images? It doesn't fit his pattern."

"Maybe he put it where it would go if it *was* registered," said Val.

"Then a librarian or attentive student might notice and look into it," said Cal. "That's what surprises me about the code on Senior Walk. It was high-effort but sloppy, leaving those clues out in the open."

"Like you keep saying, though, he wants to be found."

"True. But I get the feeling Senior Walk was his *magnum opus*. And for some reason he started early."

"What makes you say that?" Val asked.

"Because everything else *is* hidden: the boxes in Spotsylvania and Colorado, the Facebook pages; even this book. But those stars in Arkansas are right there for all to see. It's sloppy, and our man is anything but."

Val pondered that thought as she searched the fantasy and science fiction stacks on the second floor while Cal tackled the research and technology sections on the third. She had just double-checked the shelf where "Dahlgren" should have been in historical fiction when something caught her eye.

Banners for the Summer Tween Reading Marathon adorned one section of the large room. In the center sat a table full of wizard, vampire, and dystopian adventure stories. On a lectern at the end of the table lay an open book—a dictionary from the look of it. A small sign above it read "Not sure what that word means? Look it UP!"

What tween would use a dictionary instead of an iPhone? But the small plastic placard under the dictionary seized Val's attention.

It said, "For Library Use Only. Do not Remove."

Val pulled out her phone to find the closest Walmart.

✻ ✻ ✻

Val returned from her quick errand with a cup of coffee in each hand and a plastic bag dangling from her wrist. She found Cal on the third floor near the top of a ladder looking through a yellowed book with a cracked leather cover.

"No time for reading," she teased him. "We're in a library, you know?"

He smiled down at her. "What are you up to?"

"You know how sometimes I get a flash of insight, and then I get indecisive. But then I think 'WWCCD' and then everything's OK?" She said, handing him a coffee.

"Miss, are you trying to get laid?" he asked, failing to keep a straight face. "Because this is an excellent way to go about it."

She winked at him. "Later. For now, hear me out."

Cal climbed down, his face amused but attentive.

"So I was downstairs looking through some of the fiction books," she narrated while he sipped from the steaming cup. "And I saw this dictionary. I wouldn't have given it a second thought, except it had a little plastic sign that said, 'For Library Use Only.' Now, I don't know why, but my intuition fired up. So I asked myself 'What would Calvin Cooper do?'"

"What *would* I do?"

"You tell me."

His eyes lit up. "Dictionaries can't be checked out. That's why he gave the same clue for all the libraries! He probably underlined some letters. No that would be too obvious. He probably—"

Val reached into the bag and pulled out a pair of flashlights: *UV* flashlights.

Cal's smile grew.

A few minutes later, they met back up in a fourth-floor study room. Val hefted a dictionary from its temporary place on a chair. "It was on the first-floor reference books shelf. I checked two others on the tables before I found it."

Cal chuckled. "You had better luck than me."

"Flick the switch and take a look."

Cal turned off the lights and made his way to the desk with his UV light. He flipped the dictionary to one of two pages she'd marked with scrap paper; the one that contained the definition of 'burn.' When he shined the light on the page, two previously unseen words appeared:

UNDER DESK

He flipped to the page with the "jester" entry and found:

Fourth Floor

"Not this desk, I take it?" said Cal.

"I already looked," she said. "But there are a few other study rooms on this floor, along with six classrooms and a couple of microfilm rooms. I think we can rule out the classrooms; it'd be too easy for someone to chance upon the book there."

"Let's check them just in case."

Val nodded. "You take the west side. I'll stay on this half."

They split up. Val's already racing heart thudded in her ears as she searched the rooms on the fourth floor's east side. She was under the instructor's desk in one classroom when a male voice rumbling from the entrance almost gave her a coronary.

"What are you doing in here?"

Val peeked over the desktop, dreading to see the tall, brawny figure Raymond Bendall had spied at Kayla Reynolds' forest grave. Instead, a maintenance man stood in the doorway, his arms crossed over his jumpsuit.

"I dropped a pen," Val squeaked as her face heated.

"Sorry to startle you." He pointed to the fluorescent light fixtures in the drop ceiling, "but I gotta change some bulbs."

Val eased herself to her feet. "No problem. I'll go study somewhere else."

"You know there's study rooms, right?" he said. "A couple just three doors down."

"Thanks," she mumbled. "Excuse me." *At least I still look young enough to pass for a student* she thought as she left.

Val slipped into the last study room on the library's east side. She crawled under a desk, but the creak of the door opening interrupted her search.

"Dropped another one," Val announced with a forced giggle. "I am all thumbs today."

"You dropped what?" Cal asked from the doorway.

Val stood—her face hot again, but not with shame. A simple motion of Cal's head told her to follow him. She stifled the emotion bubbling up inside her and complied.

Cal led the way to one of the microfilm rooms. "People have been coming and going sporadically. So let's get this done and get out of here."

He pulled a compact screwdriver set from his jacket pocket and entered the dim room. Four fiberboard-topped sheet metal desks, each with drawers inside and a microfilm reader on top, waited within.

Cal chose the one on the far left, crawled under it on his back, and turned his phone light on. "Hon," he whispered, "can you hold this for a second?"

Val crouched down and took the phone.

"Shine it right here," Cal pointed to a gap between the drawers and the back of the desk. There, a metal box had been screwed to the underside of the desktop.

Val's stomach fluttered with anticipation. "Is this it?"

"It's not part of the microfilm reader," Cal said as he unscrewed the box. "And none of the other desks have one." He removed the last screw, got up, and placed the box on the desk. The top was open, revealing a white cloth-wrapped object inside. Cal moved the bundle to a small zipper bag he'd brought along.

"Here," he said as he handed Val the bag. "Anyone who sees this will think it's a purse. Best if you carry it out."

As they walked out of the library, Val couldn't get rid of the feeling that she was holding a live hand grenade.

The Mousetrap Manifesto - The Tome and the Vessel

THE MOUSETRAP MURDERS us all.

Even the Fulcrum had been murdered, only to be reforged as another.
   For his original form was strong in many ways but weak in others.
   This reforging required a crucible to attain ultimate purity; greatness.
   And it required a vessel.
   The first came to him in the form of a book—a scripture. One that had been written just for him. One that had sought him out.
   He'd happened upon the scripture one day, almost a week after they had arrested the young man in Colorado. He had enjoyed his time there. Rural areas offered tranquility not found in more urban locales. He'd even mused about retiring there when his work was done. As news of the arrest rippled throughout the small college town, the Fulcrum—still known by most as Alastor St. John—took a stroll down the streets of Alamosa.
   The Fulcrum wandered into a bookstore run by a red-eyed stoner he'd gotten to know. He nodded to the man and walked the aisles in a slow, deliberate manner.

"Hey, Professor," the proprietor motioned to the display case at the back of the store. "Look what I picked up yesterday." The stoner picked up a book he had stashed behind the case. "Not sure if I got gypped or what. But it looked cool, so I figured what the heck."

Cauldron of Empires, the book's title read, by N.R. Dahlgren.

The shop owner handed it to him. "Have you ever heard of it?"

Alastor shook his head and flipped to the introduction. "There is a war coming to America. And it is coming from within," it began.

"Some dude passing through said he picked it up in Cali," the stoner confided. "Said it was real rare and valuable. Well, he let it go for seventy-five bucks …"

Alastor kept reading as the shopkeeper rambled.

"I couldn't find anything on it, not even on Yahoo or AltaVista. It—"

"I'll give you a hundred dollars for it." Alastor snapped the book shut and stared the man in the eye.

He brought his new purchase home and spent hours devouring it.

> *America even now is at a crossroads. Its final form has yet to be determined. But one thing is clear to anyone paying attention. Those who have been in control will not be for long. The flame of Revolution, once thought extinguished, has been smoldering, fuming, waiting to catch fire once again. And from its ashes the Sons of Africa, I think, will rise and take the scepter. This will come at a great cost and will require a great spark to signal the downtrodden people of America to stand up and rebel against their White oppressors. It will require those under the Plight of the Poor to unshackle themselves and take flight.*

He realized then that he was the spark.

He would start the revolution.

Before, he had chosen his morsels and his mice to lash out at a broken system. He had wanted to reveal the inequity of a so-called just society and be a mover of change.

But the book had changed that vision. It had allowed him to see that he could be the Prime Mover toward the future Dahlgren wrote of. The book lit a fire that burned away the impurities of his randomness and set him on a defined course.

But to attain his position; to grasp what he so desperately sought, he needed to become something more. He needed to shed the identity of Alastor St. John and put on the great man, the King, which the book spoke of.

He needed a Vessel.

A few weeks later, he had accepted another position in another sociology department. After a few months, he began mentoring at-risk foster kids.

All the while he searched, and he waited.

He found his Vessel in 1999: a tall but insecure Black boy who'd been in a dozen foster homes. He was almost seventeen when Alastor took him in.

By 2001, Alastor St. John was dead—burned beyond recognition in a car crash on a lonely stretch of highway between Lubbock and Dallas.

From the ashes emerged the Vessel, the newest incarnation of the Fulcrum.

He was now the Father and the Son.

And he was also the Spark that would light the flame over which the Cauldron of the United States would burn off its impurities.

star, hand painted in black. Markings on some of the points in a dried crimson substance made Val jump.

Her eyes drifted down the hidden compartment to a set of business cards paperclipped under the star.

The Defective
The Vagrant
The Trucker
The Runner
The Warrior
The Weakling
The Wanderer

Folded up at the back of the set was a small square of paper. Val unfolded it to find a handwritten note:
Come at last, o Providence, to the twisted halls of my Dreadful Kingdom

3288 Thornbrook Hollows Road

※ ※ ※

Searching for the address online turned up one oddity after another. Cal found it was in a gated neighborhood on the outskirts of Columbia. The Google Maps street view was blurred out, as it was in every other online map service. The house's layout was available though, and it showed a large open area in the basement.

But every single resource he and Val consulted to identify the owner drew a blank.

Cal rang Carrington.

"I'll come up with a name in a day or two," the detective said on speakerphone.

"What do you think of the symbol we found in the book?" Cal asked him.

"I think it jibes with what you found in Arkansas. There are six sets of murder victims and supposed killers. And six of the eight points on that star are marked. Of those, the first, second, and fourth have the additional mark above. Crossing the T, you could say. If we look at the men convicted of the killings, King, Latimore, and Oliver have all been executed. They were the first, second, and fourth in chronological order."

"It's a scoreboard," said Cal.

"And he's planning on two more," Val said.

"He's not gonna get them," said Carrington. "We know where he is."

"Do we call the police yet?" Val asked with audible reluctance.

Carrington sighed. "Like I said before, it's your call. But I'd wait until we have this guy's name. If we can pin down his whereabouts over the years, even better. We have to leave the local cops and the feds with no doubt. Scratch that—we have to leave them no choice."

It was Cal's turn to broach an uncomfortable but necessary

subject. "How many hours will that kind of proof take? I don't want my next check to bounce."

"Don't worry about it," said Carrington. "In this particular ham and egg sandwich, I've gone from chicken to pig."

Cal shared a smile with his wife. "We appreciate your commitment, Ted."

Carrington laughed. "All I ask is that when you sign over the movie rights, add a clause saying that Brad Pitt plays me."

"The only question now," said Val, "is how do we get a closer look at a house in a gated neighborhood?"

Cal winked at her. "We'll have to get creative."

※ ※ ※

"I think this is your sly way of getting an early birthday present," Val said as the drone loitered over a gate off the wooded path behind Thornbrook Hollows Estates.

"You'll get a turn, too." Cal said as he maneuvered the drone closer to the path with the controller. "It's beginner friendly."

Val folded her arms. "Thanks, but since my brother's life is on the line, I'll leave it to the guy who's spent untold weekends flying those things with his friends."

Each gate in the fence separating the subdivision from paved trail had electronic locks that required a PIN to open. Cal and Val stood in a nearby clearing, waiting for residents to open the gate. When one did, Cal would zoom the drone's high-resolution camera in to capture the code.

"How unethical is this, I wonder?" Val asked. She had a small notebook and a pen ready to take down the numbers her husband called out.

"I doubt they'll blacklist us from Heaven for this," Cal said as he studied the controller's display. "Looks like someone's back from a jog. Get ready to write this down."

Val jotted down the numbers as Cal read them from his screen. Along with the others they'd grabbed in the past hour, that made three PINs capable of unlocking the gate.

"We should use a different code each time," Cal said.

Val nodded. "No point being sloppy."

Cal had also used the drone to get a bird's-eye view of the subdivision. The only guards were posted at the two main vehicle entrances. Lucky for them, the house they were interested in was on the far side of the neighborhood.

Cal recalled the drone with its Come Home feature, packed it in its carrying case, and stowed it in the rental car. He and Val donned hats and sunglasses, and then made their way to the nearest gate. When they were sure the path was clear, Cal entered the first PIN in the keypad. The gate swung open, and they went through.

Most of the houses they passed had similar brick exteriors and dark shingles. Val pointed out superfluous columns and fake shutters on some, which she called "gaudy."

Cal was on the lookout for something else. "Only a few have security cameras. And those are mounted just over the front door."

"To see when their packages come from Amazon," Val chuckled.

"Not a lot of porch pirates in this neighborhood," said Cal. "Even without the gates and the guards, this is one of Columbia's safer areas."

The Thornbrook neighborhood boasted not just low crime, but a high average income, judging by the size of the houses. Teslas and Bimmers graced the driveways, and Cal even spotted a Maserati Ghibli.

"We better be careful," Val whispered. "One of the neighbors might report a suspicious Mexican to the police."

"Not to worry," Cal quipped, "you've got your designated White chaperone."

Her smile failed to hide the low-level anxiety Cal had sensed from her all morning.

3288 Thornbrook Hollows stood at the end of a cul-de-sac. A two-story brick affair like the rest, its fence enclosed a half-acre of manicured lawn which glistened from recent watering.

"It seems downright idyllic," said Val.

But there were tells of hidden secrets as clear as a poker player licking his lips. Blackout curtains hung behind every window, despite the white Venetian blinds. The fanlight over the front door was blocked with what looked like a black garbage bag. And Cal counted six security cameras mounted around the home.

"No one looking in, and someone always looking out," he said.

They made multiple loops around the house, keeping a cautious distance so as to avoid the cameras. And they took their time, so even if they were spotted, they would look like a neighborhood couple on a long walk.

After a few passes, they determined the cameras had a blind spot on the house's garage side. An adjacent empty lot overgrown with saplings gave an approach angle hidden from prying eyes. From the vacant lot, they got a better look at the side where the floor plan located the basement stairs. But the blacked out windows denied them a view of the large room.

"If all else fails," said Cal, "we'll have to get inside. All we need is a sliver of evidence tying whoever lives there to the rest of our clues."

"I know," Val said. "I'd risk jail myself if it would help free Julian."

The garage door whirred. Cal and Val took cover behind a small tree at the back of the empty lot. A black Acura, or maybe a Lexus, backed into the street. Its tinted windows hid the driver as it drove off.

A moment later the garage door began its gradual descent.

"What are those? Cal pointed to what looked like a set of handles on the garage floor.

Val shook her head. "At least we know someone lives there."

Cal produced the gadget he'd bought with the drone and the burner phones and placed it among the underbrush.

"What is that?" Val whispered even though they were alone.

"RFID skimmer," Cal said as he aligned the flat TV antenna-like device with the blind spot in front of the garage. "It will intercept any signal sent by a transmitter in range—say a garage door opener remote."

"It'll block the signal?"

"No, that's the beauty of it. The skimmer picks up the signal without interrupting the transaction. And in the process it steals the information that's transmitted."

"Which I'm guessing is illegal."

"Yes it is. So let's only use the signals for the garage door and the security system—and only if there's no other choice."

"Fine by me," said Val.

"We've done what we can do for now." Cal gently took hold of her arm and guided her toward the sidewalk.

"What about the skimmer?"

"I'll get it later tonight," said Cal. "Let's be gone before whoever that was gets back."

They returned to their rental car and switched their phones out of airplane mode.

Cal frowned at his screen. "Looks like I missed a call from Ted."

"Me, too," Val said, "and a text."

Cal called the investigator back and put him on speakerphone.

"Thanks for returning my calls," Carrington said.

"I take it you found something," said Cal.

"Is that beautiful wife of yours there?"

"I'm here, Ted," Val smiled to stifle her nerves. "You're on speaker."

"Good, because I want to ask if the name 'Edwin McMichael' rings a bell."

Val bit her lip in concentration, then her eyes lit up. "From CrimeMeet."

"What?" said Cal.

"One of the speakers at the crime convention I went to in Chicago," she blurted.

Carrington went on. "Dr. Edwin McMichael is a professor of criminal justice at the University of Missouri. And he owns the house at 3288 Thornbrook Hollows Road."

Cal's heart lodged in his throat. "Not that I doubt you, but given the delicacy of the situation, are you sure this is our guy?"

"McMichael has been a professor of criminal justice for almost thirty-five years," said Carrington. "He started as an assistant professor in St. Louis and became an associate professor at two other Midwest colleges. For the last twenty years, he's taught at the University of Missouri."

Val's face fell. "Nothing in Virginia, Arkansas, or Colorado?"

"To supplement his professorship," Carrington said, "he does the lecture circuit and guest speaking at various colleges and universities. He's been very busy over the years."

"Which would make travel to all of the murder locations easy," said Cal.

"He had the means and opportunity," the investigator said. "And get this: He's a vocal opponent of the death penalty."

"Giving real examples of innocent men getting executed is a good way to discredit the death penalty," Cal thought aloud. "So good, he might have decided to make some."

"That's speculation," said Carrington, "but it is a motive."

"What about the other side of the coin?" Val asked. "Do his teaching or speaking engagements give him alibis for any of the killings?"

"Not that I've found so far," Carrington said.

"Just one problem," said Cal. "It doesn't quite fit our guy's M.O. He's calculating and cautious, but he's also patient. The murders are all seven years apart, except the last one. Just picking a victim and someone to frame could take him weeks or months. Could he do that while teaching in another state?"

"That might actually explain the long intervals between murders," Carrington said. "He plans, then he waits for the perfect opportunity and grabs it. As a guest lecturer he could be at a university for a few weeks or a whole semester. That would give him time to set it all up."

"Maybe." Cal left his lingering doubts unspoken and said,

"Thanks for everything, Ted."

"I should thank you for the excitement," said Carrington. "It's been a while since I've been leaned on by the feds."

"That's why we're going radio silent for a while," said Cal.

After a beat Carrington said, "Just tell me you don't plan to do anything stupid."

"You brought us a solid lead," said Cal, "but we have to make sure for ourselves."

He looked to Val, who nodded in solidarity.

"No use getting someone else involved," Cal went on, "especially with the bloodhound gang breathing down your neck."

"'The bloodhound gang,'" Carrington laughed, "I like that. Just remember, they've got your scent, too. So don't wake the dogs."

Cal exchanged a look with his wife. "We're more interested in the wolf."

TWENTY-_WO

THE UNIVERSITY OF Missouri's website confirmed that McMichael wasn't teaching summer courses. And the department secretary had told them over the phone that he only had office hours one day a week from 1 pm to 3 pm.

Cal had kept in contact with Mose and Dwayne, which gave him the idea to have Dwayne meet with McMichael, posing as a student. It would keep the guy out of the house and in a public space, in case they decided to confront him.

So Dwayne drove up from Arkansas to help. And he gave them the pleasant surprise of bringing Jasmine along. They met up at the hotel and made a list of questions for McMichael. Besides some typical criminology topics, they sprinkled in some questions about his past to check against Carrington's snooping.

Still, McMichael largely remained a mystery. They'd hadn't even gotten a good look at the man in person. He never set foot outside his front or back door. How he disposed of his trash remained an enigma.

Cal had glimpsed the Doctor's profile one morning as he drove past but could only confirm that the driver was tall and male. Both attributes fit Raymond Bendall's description. So did McMichael's interviews on the web. His YouTube clips depicted him as an inch or two taller than Cal, who stood six-two. McMichael didn't look especially strong, though.

"The suits he always wears could hide his muscles," Cal

had speculated.

"And it's been seven years since Virginia," Val had said. "McMichael is in his sixties now. Even if he's stayed in shape, he'll have lost muscle mass due to age."

This plan would also expose McMichael to direct observation. Cal wanted to see who they were up against in the flesh.

✳ ✳ ✳

The best-laid plans of mice and men often go awry.

Cal was parked on the street outside the Thornbrook Hollows Estates' main gates. Val had taken a lookout position near the house. Having surveilled McMichael's place for almost a week—and having started following him when he left—they were sure they had his routine.

"You ready, Cal? He just left the house."

"Yeah, I'm ready. But he's way early. Will you text Dwayne and Jasmine to make sure they're in place?"

According to public records the Doctor had divorced a few years back, and his kids were grown. But a girlfriend would have added a major complication. Luckily, they'd seen no indication of any other occupants.

He only left by car and had so far driven to the same place: the police station.

"If only those cops knew how close they were to a serial killer," Cal mused aloud.

"Well, they obviously don't," said Val. "And his relationship with the local PD makes this a lot riskier."

"A lot of serial killers hang around cops. This guy's just taken it a step further. It's a good bet he knows the police in every town where he's killed someone."

"Meaning he's poisoned the well everywhere we'd want to go to for help."

"Yeah," Cal said. "I have to admit I'm not optimistic about the cops giving us their full cooperation."

"Are you telling me that Plan B is our only shot?"

"I'm telling you that as close as we are to the end, we're going to have to be careful not to trip up. Because I'm not sure if there's a police department involved in this that would just as soon bury it than admit their involvement."

"Then we might need a Plan C."

The professor's black sedan stopped at the Thornbrook Hollows Estates guard shack. As soon as the barrier lifted, it proceeded down the street past Cal. He gave it a few seconds' lead time and followed the car toward the university.

He had been following the sedan for a few minutes when Cal's phone buzzed. It was a text from Dwayne. Cal was about to call him back when the black sedan merged into the turn lane, made a quick U-turn, and headed back the way they'd come.

At a loss for what to do next, Cal cast about for ideas. He remembered Dwayne's text and, trying to keep one eye on the road, he read the full message.

"McMichael isn't here. He's been in Australia for a month."

On instinct, Cal swerved the rental car to the left, cutting off several other vehicles and almost getting sideswiped before screeching into the turn lane. His own U-turn was stymied by a stream of oncoming traffic.

Australia? Sweat trickled down Cal's forehead as he waited for an opening in the endless line of cars. *What the hell is he doing there? And who have we been following?*

He dialed Dwayne, and the second the young man picked up, Cal said, "Australia? Are you sure?"

"Yeah," Dwayne groaned. "The secretary you talked to was a temp. This other one said—"

"She's 100 percent positive there's no way he's still in town?" Cal said on the unfamiliar edge of panic.

"Yes, she said she spoke to him this morning from Sydney. What should we do now?"

"Go back to the hotel and wait for us," Cal said. "If we're not there in three hours, head home. I'll explain later."

He called Val and knew the second she answered that

something was wrong.

"I'm so sorry, Cal," she breathed. "I'm in the house."

"You're *where*?"

"I disabled the alarm, but he must have rearmed it with his phone."

Shit! As he sped back to Thornbrook Hollows, a stream of silent prayers processed through Cal's mind.

Both he and Val would need them.

※ ※ ※

Minutes earlier, Val had hung up with Cal and texted Jasmine to confirm she and Dwayne were on their way to the meeting. Then she looked around the obscenely neat garage. *I hope I know what I'm doing. And I hope Cal forgives me.*

She had snuck into the garage as the door was closing—after making sure McMichael's car was out of sight. She had tried to act natural in case any neighbors were out and hoped they'd been right about the cameras' blind spot.

Now, Val approached the door to the kitchen. She stopped and held her breath for a few seconds to calm her nerves.

Why am I doing this? She could have waited for Dwayne and Jasmine to make another appointment, and instead of following the professor Cal would be here with her. That would have given them hours to search the house.

That had been their plan. It had made the most sense.

But she was here now, and McMichael would be gone a long while—Dwayne's questions would make sure of that. He would text her the second he was done, and she would be out of here with plenty of time to spare.

So she put on a black balaclava in case there were any cameras inside and entered the code Cal had skimmed into the keypad by the door. It gave a muted beep. She tried the knob, half-expecting it to be locked. But it turned with no trouble, so she opened the door. A single beep sounded from somewhere in the middle of the house. Val paused to slow her racing heart and stepped into the kitchen.

Thanks to the thick blackout curtains, deep gloom filled the interior. Val groped the wall and felt a light switch. She flipped it to reveal a kitchen without character or creature comforts. The countertops lay bare, and the only appliances were a refrigerator, a stove, and a microwave.

It looks unlived in.

She closed the door and was about to set the alarm to "Home" when a buzz made her jump.

Just my phone! It was a text from Cal, saying McMichael was at the gate.

"Be careful," she texted back before proceeding into the living room. Like the garage and the kitchen, it was bare bones. A single sofa sat at the far end before an old entertainment center, upon which stood a small flat screen TV. Dozens of old VHS tapes filled the shelves beneath. From that distance she couldn't make out any titles, though most looked like home movies.

But no pictures adorned the walls or the end table. Nor did anything else give her personal details about McMichael that might tie him to the murders.

What struck her most was that while the house looked like new construction, all the furniture was old and worn. The sparseness of the rooms and the musty smell gave her the creeps.

Not how I would have guessed a well-known professor would live.

Val turned off the kitchen light and proceeded upstairs. She made a right into one of the guest bedrooms, switched the lights on, and got a surprise. An expensive-looking ultramodern tanning bed lay inside. Several spray tan containers cluttered a small table next to it. Otherwise, it was as barren as the other rooms: nothing on the walls, no extraneous furniture; sterile.

Out of the corner of her eye, Val caught the outline of a man standing to her left. She stifled her scream when it turned out to be the torso of a mannequin. Several irregular leather patches were pinned to its head.

Having seen more than she cared to, Val backed out of there

and approached the master suite at the end of the hall. Opening the door a crack, she got an instant sense of wrongness. Of dread.

Get out. Get out right now, Val.

But she shook her head to ease the knot in her stomach and opened the door the rest of the way. A small lamp at the end of the room cast dim red light over tall square shapes. She flicked the light switch to find the bedroom full of stacked boxes. And the earthy smell of old paper.

The boxes surrounded a single bed in the room's center. A narrow clear path allowed navigation from the door to the bedside and the dresser next to it.

Three framed pictures stood atop the dresser. Val picked her way to them, and her sense of dread increased when she saw the face captured in each photo.

That's not McMichael.

It was a hulking black man that dwarfed the photos' other subjects. In the first, he wore a graduation gown. In the second, he bowed to receive an award from a police officer. The last showed him in front of an old barn. All seemed superficially normal. Yet each picture held some element that felt off.

It was the man's face.

Vitiligo ...

Loud beeping from downstairs activated her flight reflex. Val turned and ran into a stack of boxes. She struggled to keep her balance and grabbed at the stack to her right as the one she'd hit teetered. Both stacks fell, pulling her down with them.

Her heart pounding in time with the frantic beeping, Val climbed back to her feet.

I forgot the alarm! She scrambled out of the room, hitting the light switch on her way out. The beeping sped up as she stumbled down the night-black hallway.

The motion detectors would be switching on at any moment. Shit, how am I gonna get out of here?

Val traversed the dark hallway and rushed down the stairs

to the first floor.
Can't go back to the garage. But where …?
The plan.
The basement.

She would take the stairs down there and wait. He'd come in through the kitchen and disarm the alarm. Then she could slip out the back.

Val barreled down the ground floor hallway, hoping in her memory of the layout. The beeping had quickened to an almost constant tone. Running her hand along the right wall as she sprinted, she felt a door frame and stopped. Val scrabbled for the knob, turned it, and almost tumbled down the stairs as the door swung away from her. But she lurched through without falling and slammed it behind her.

As she stood with her back to the door, her phone's buzzing pierced her adrenaline fog.

It was Cal.

"Okay," he said trying not to sound alarmed after she told him where she was, though she could still hear it in his voice, "can you get to the basement? Like we planned?"

"Yes, I'm on the stairs leading down there. The motion detectors are on."

"Are there cameras inside?"

"I haven't seen any yet, but there might be."

"Get down to the basement as soon as he disarms the system. He may re-arm it as soon as he's in, so be quick. The basement door should have another keypad. You remember the code?"

"Yeah." She bit her lip to keep from bursting into tears.

"The second you're at the door," said Cal, "disable the alarm and get out. I'll meet you."

"See you there." She doubted her words even as she spoke them.

※ ※ ※

Cal resisted the urge go floor it down the suburban streets.

Getting pulled over would cost precious time Val didn't have. He settled for doing thirty-nine in a twenty-five, though he sped up as soon as the security gates were in sight.

The black Lexus was already rolling through.

Cal turned onto a parallel street. He fought rising anxiety as he half-drifted around two roundabouts and sped to a small lot near the walking trail.

The nearest entry gate off the walking trail was about a quarter mile from the parking lot, and then the house was at least another half mile from there. *More like a mile if I'm being honest*, he thought.

As he was parking, he went over the list of actions he needed to perform in his head, knowing that any delay could put his wife in danger, but also knowing that going in empty-handed would be foolish as well. He stopped the car in a jolt, popped the trunk, grabbed what he needed, locked the car, and sprinted to the walking path gate.

Once through the gate, Cal dashed down the sidewalk at a full tilt.

Breathe, he told himself. *You won't do any good if you're gassed when you get there.*

The path made a sharp left up ahead. But there was a shortcut behind one of the houses that would cut thirty seconds off his trip.

On his way down the gentle slope, the cylinder in his hand slipped, and he had to slow down to regain his grip.

Focus, he thought as he pumped his legs harder. *Val, I'm coming. God gird me with Your strength for whatever is to come!*

* * *

The garage door rumbled as Val descended the dark stairs. She steeled herself to open the door and cross the basement as soon as the security system was disarmed.

Another hateful rumble coursed through the ceiling as the garage door closed. Val waited. For ten seconds. Thirty. Two minutes. After what felt like half an hour, cold dread encroached on her controlled panic.

What if he's coming in through the basement door? She shivered at the thought of running into the giant from the upstairs photos.

It's him, the man Raymond Bendall saw burying Kayla and carrying Julian like a rag doll.

They'd been wrong about McMichael. And this mountain of a man had come reckoning.

A muffled beep came from above, and hinges creaked. Val eased the basement door open, slipped through, and shut it behind her.

Darkness thicker than that of the rooms above engulfed her. She felt as if she were suffocating; could sense objects on every side. Her outstretched hand touched a rough wooden shape. She barked her shin on something hard and fell in the dark.

Val stood up, rubbed her sore shin, and turned on her cell phone light. It shone on two enormous tables covered with dozens of pictures and file folders. She only glanced at them as she passed between the two tables toward the door at the back of the room. The keypad was there, but so was a plank a foot wide and several inches thick, which barred the door.

Heavy footsteps shook the ceiling, though Val couldn't tell if they were coming from the first or second floor. Hands trembling, she pulled up the disarm code on her phone and punched it into the keypad. She moved to stuff the phone in her pocket and missed, but let it fall and tried instead to lift the plank from the steel brackets that flanked the door.

Not sure I can do this … she realized as her muscles strained yet the plank didn't budge.

Upstairs, the footsteps paused. All of a sudden they broke into a run. On the verge of outright panic, Val pivoted to the hinge side. She heaved with all her strength, and the plank moved, only to snag on something. A frantic burst of effort dislodged the bar, which she lifted free to slide down the opposite bracket and thud to the floor.

The footsteps pounded down the basement stairs. Val fumbled with the first of three deadbolts as the door from the stairwell flew open. The click of a switch flooded the room with bright light, and Val turned both remaining deadbolts blind. A sharp crack sounded somewhere behind her, and an explosion cratered the wall to her right, showering her with concrete chips.

She tried the knob, but the lock was still engaged. A fleeting glance to her left showed a man hurdling over the table with pistol in hand, knocking papers everywhere.

The flat lock button disengaged. Val turned the knob and pulled the door open. Free air came streaming into the suffocating abyss.

A massive hand grabbed the back of Val's collar and slung her back. Her head snapped forward so fast, her neck cracked in her ears. She hit the floor and skidded to a stop against a table leg. The back door slammed shut, and the lights went off.

Cal! A torrent of emotions inundated her. But one thought cut through the noise: *Gotta stop him from locking the door!*

"Cauldron of Empires!" she cried over the ringing in her ears.

The giant froze.

"Cauldron of Empires!" she yelled again, with even more force.

He turned from the door. Her fallen phone underlit the mottled face leering down at her, giving it a monstrous cast. The giant's arms dropped to his sides. His silenced high-caliber pistol looked like a toy in his bearish hand.

God please, she prayed, *despite my selfish pride, spare my husband.*

A crooked smile spread across the monster's face. "Now how do we know that name?" he said in a sweet, controlled voice.

"I'm with law enforcement," she improvised. "We know all about you."

"Oh, do we now?" the figure took a step toward her.

Val scooted clear of the table and tried to stand. A sharp pain shot up her leg, forcing her to use a chair for support. *I think I broke something.*

"We know about Virginia," she said, just managing to keep

her voice from trembling. "And Colorado. And your message in Arkansas."

"Impressive. But I fail t'be convinced. No, li'l girl. I think you all alone. If you really knew who I was, you wouldn't be here. Not without a SWAT team, anyhow. No, I think all you know right now is what deep shit you in, and you just a-treadin' water."

He took another step in her direction. Val hobbled back, but he aimed the gun at her head.

"That's quite enough," he chided her. "Now, you take that mask off your head so I take a look at you before I peel your face off your skull."

The callous ease with which he spoke aroused more sadness than fear in Val. *My children will grow up without me, for my pride.* She reached up as if to remove the mask.

A flicker of movement behind the giant told Val to lunge back. But as she started her jump, her knee gave out. There was noise, a rush of white, another crack and a muzzle flash.

It's not supposed to be like this, it's all backwards.

Darkness took her.

TWENTY-T_REE

CAL THOUGHT HE'D been running all-out until he heard the muffled but unmistakable gunshot. His ears couldn't pinpoint the source, but his racing heart spurred him toward 3288 Thornbrook Hollows Road. He flew around the corner of the house and dashed for the outdoor stairway as the basement door banged shut.

The cement landing was empty.

Suppressing the urge to charge in, Cal forced himself to creep down the steps. He took a deep breath. His heart's thumping slowed, and he heard Val's muffled shout. A second voice answered, though he couldn't hear the words it spoke.

Cal gripped the red canister in one hand and placed the other on the doorknob. If it was locked, he'd have to bust through, losing precious time. If it was unlocked, just turning it might alert the owner.

More talking filtered out. Judging by the drop in volume, Val had lured the guy away from the door.

Please God, Cal prayed one last time. He tried the knob. It turned without resistance, and he eased the door open a sliver.

"... that mask off your head so I can take a look at you before I peel your face off your skull," a calm voice drifted out.

Cal pulled his fire extinguisher's pin and kicked the door with all his might. The stranger's broad back met him, and Cal discharged the canister's contents at it. A suppressed gunshot reverberated from concrete walls, Val yelped in pain, and a body dropped to the floor.

Fury warred with Cal's despair. *Too late!*

He charged as the ursine figure started to turn. Fire suppressant still hung heavy in the darkened room. But daylight pouring through the doorway lit the lumbering figure like a street lamp in dense fog.

The gunman raised his pistol, but Cal sidestepped, and the shot went wide. Cal swung the canister backhanded into the man's gun hand. The weapon went flying into the shadow-drenched basement.

Cal dove at the giant. He ducked under long, clutching arms and thrust the extinguisher into his opponent's throat. That move would have finished most fights, but the beast shook it off and enveloped Cal's chest. He lifted Cal off his feet and squeezed the air from his lungs.

Cal still held the fire extinguisher, but it was useless while the man had his arm pinned above him. Cal forced his head back as far as he could manage, and then brought it forward, smashing his forehead into the man's nose. This collision produced a sickening crunch, but still the man held on.

Cal repeated the headbutt, and the crushing grapple loosened. Seizing the slight opportunity, he held the fire extinguisher's nozzle an inch from the stranger's face and emptied the container's contents into his bellowing mouth.

The brute dropped Cal and staggered back, retching aerosolized powder. Cal took a knee and gulped down chemical-tasting air. He recovered while the stranger leaned against the far wall, supporting himself with one hand.

Cal approached the heaving beast. The giant rounded on him, swinging a stout plank that missed Cal's head by a hair. As Cal reeled, the stranger brought the plank back, holding it like a bat.

"Come on, friend," the giant wheezed. "Earn your place in history next t'me if you dare."

Another figure appeared at the doorway and pointed what looked like a gun at the big man. But it emitted a small spark instead of a muzzle flash. Two taser probes embedded themselves in the large man's face. But the giant just growled and swung the makeshift club at his new assailant.

"Oh fuck!" shouted Carrington. He ducked, and the heavy plank shattered against the door frame just above his head.

Carrington launched himself at the big man, who stumbled back a step. Cal jumped on the monster's back and wrapped an arm around his neck in a choke hold. Though dogpiled by two men over six feet, the brute pushed Ted away and decked him in the jaw, sending him reeling.

Cal maintained pressure on the giant's neck. He backed up, crushing Cal against the wall. It took all of Cal's strength to hold on.

The lights blazed to life, blinding Cal for a second. The man raised a hand to shield his eyes while beating Cal's shoulder and head with the other.

Carrington tackled the giant's knees. Cal let go as they buckled, dropping the big man on his back. Cal pressed his knee into the brute's face and held his right arm back as Ted held down his left.

A ripping noise came from behind. Cal turned to see the most glorious sight imaginable.

Val looked like an angel in the lingering haze, despite the blood trickling down the side of her face. She scooted close, dragging her right leg behind her.

"Mertz," she said, "hold him steady."

Knowing better than to ask any questions, Cal forced all his weight on the stranger. Val poured the contents of a container into a black rag in her hand and she said, "You two, hold your breath."

Cal and Ted turned and closed their mouths as Val pressed the cloth over the big man's nose and mouth. His struggling steadily weakened until he went limp.

Val whispered in his ear. "Night, night, mother*fucker*."

"Where'd you get that?" Ted asked, the side of his face already swelling.

"The chloroform?" Val sat back with a heavy exhale. "There's four more bottles of it back there."

"Ted," Cal said as he gathered his wife in his arms, "would you close the door? Otherwise, we might alert someone besides a private eye in Virginia."

Carrington stood and dusted himself off. "Guess I owe you that—and an explanation." He went to lock up.

When Ted returned, Cal extended a hand. The investigator took it.

"You saved my ass, Ted. You saved my wife. Thank you, my friend."

Ted waved it off. "I almost didn't save anything. This dude —who, by the way, is not Edwin McMichael—almost took my head off."

"Yeah," Cal said, wrapping both arms around his wife again, "we know."

"I'm sorry hon," Val said on the verge of tears. "I should have listened to you. Instead I almost got us killed."

Though furious that Val had risked her life, Cal's gratitude that the Lord had protected her dwarfed his anger. "How bad are you hurt?"

"Don't deflect," she said in her stubborn way. "I'm asking your forgiveness."

"And I'm offering it," Cal said, holding her face in his hand. "Now, how bad are you hurt?"

"I'm a mess," she said. "I think I've got a broken knee or a torn ACL. Plus I hit my head on the way down and blacked out for a minute."

"I'm gonna have to trade you in for a new model," Cal said. "Maybe I'll try a blonde this time."

She made as if to punch him, but could only manage a giggle. Then she burst into tears and buried her head in her husband's chest.

TWENTY-FO_R

"ACCORDING TO DOCUMENTS I found in the master bedroom," Carrington told Val and Cal when he returned to the basement, "the big man's name is Maliq Henderson."

"That's what the driver's license we took off him said," Val reminded him as she sat resting her injured leg. "Did you find anything else?"

"It just so happens I did," the PI said. "Henderson had a sensor on the bedroom door. My bet is when you opened it, he got a text alert and hauled ass back here."

"So I didn't mess up too bad forgetting to set the alarm," said Val. "Still, my intuition told me not open that damn door. I should've listened."

Cal squeezed her shoulder. "Quit beating yourself up, hon. It could have gone much worse. If Dwayne and Jasmine hadn't come, I might've been at the university when Maliq came back."

"I'd be dead," she said, blunt and somber. Thoughts of Jake and Addie growing up without their mother flashed through her head again. "Did you call Dwayne and tell him to head home?"

"Yeah," said Cal. "He wanted to help some more, but I told him he should go give Mose our regards, elope with Jasmine, and keep quiet about all of this."

"Too bad he can't get his turn in the limelight," said Val. "The press would flip over a black comp sci student catching a black serial killer."

"Call me crazy," said Ted, "but I don't think our man here is African-American."

Val furled her brow. "What makes you say that?"

"You noticed the tanning bed upstairs?" Ted asked. "And the loads of tanning oil?"

"I figured he was trying to minimize the vitiligo on his face," Val said. "Tanning beds can make it worse, though."

Ted produced one of the larger swatches that had been pinned to the mannequin, crouched down, and laid it on Henderson's sleeping face. It was a perfect match for the white blotch on his left cheek. "The underside is sticky. I think he applies it when he tans. He may not even be bald, but just shaves his head and puts these patches on."

"Strange. How much longer until he comes around?" asked Cal.

"Another hour maybe," Val said. "We can dose him again if needed."

"Tempting as it is," said Cal, "let's try not to kill him."

Val glanced down at her smarting leg. "A big guy like him can take it."

"Good," said Ted. "I want to look into his movements a little more."

"What have you got so far?" asked Cal.

"He's an associate professor of sociology here in Colombia," said Ted. "I traced him back to Georgia, Virginia, then Texas, but the trail went cold. I'd like to know where he was before that."

"Why don't we ask him?" said Val.

Cal and Ted gave her wide-eyed stares.

"Look," she said, "we've got one shot at this, right? It might take weeks or months to go through this whole house, and we still may not get everything we need. At some point, somebody's gonna notice this guy missing. We have to turn him over to the authorities anyway, so let's get everything we can out of him first."

"Is that why you called me Mertz before?" Cal asked her.

"If he thinks we're cops or feds, maybe it'll loosen his lips." Val grinned at Ted. "Let's make our case undeniable, right?"

After a moment, Ted answered with a grin of his own. "Right. So what do you have in mind?"

"First," said Val, "we go shopping."

※ ※ ※

Val sat in the basement with a balaclava on her head and a temporary brace on her leg. Though propped up on a stool, the injured limb still gave her some discomfort.

Not as much as Henderson must have felt, sitting tied up and handcuffed opposite her.

Getting him off the floor and into a chair had been an ordeal in itself. The man's driver's license listed him at six foot six and 258 pounds. Cal thought that weight had to be light by at least twenty pounds after he and Ted had finally gotten him seated.

"If I'd known how big this guy was," Ted said, "I'd have brought a couple more guys."

Henderson's eyes fluttered in the glare of a shop light they'd found in a basement cabinet. A video camera recorded everything from its mount on another cabinet to the big man's right. He blinked and opened his mouth, but only slurred babble came out.

His voice is deeper than before, thought Val. *Maybe the chloroform or the extinguisher messed with his throat.*

"What y'all doing here?" Henderson asked in his previous higher register. "Get outta m-, my house."

"Mr. Henderson," Val began, "this will go much easier for you if we understand each other from the beginning."

"The fuck you talking 'bout, cunt?" he cursed. "Get outta my house."

"I told you we should have cracked him over the head, first," Cal said, playing his bad cop role. "Maybe waterboarded him."

Val glanced at her similarly masked husband. "Shut the

fuck up, Mertz." She, too, was playing a part. Not quite the good cop; more like the smug cop. Cal had insisted she play the lead. Having a woman dictate terms to him would make clear to Henderson how helpless he was.

She shifted her gaze back to Henderson. "Mr. Henderson, allow me spell a couple of things out before we go any further. You're not in control, and you never will be again. We know who you are and much of what you've done. We know about Patricia in Louisiana, Dawn in Arkansas, Felicia in Colorado, Kelsey in Texas, Kayla in Virginia, and Taylor in Georgia."

"Then you don't know shit."

Henderson struggled against his bonds. Ted's handcuffs had only just fit over the man's wrists. The rope made it impossible for him to generate any leverage, but the way it strained and groaned unnerved Val. Ted stood behind their prisoner, also wearing a balaclava and holding a shotgun they'd found in a closet. The sight gave her a measure of comfort.

After struggling a bit longer, the big man relented.

"Are you quite done, Mr. Henderson?" said Val.

"What do you want from me?" he asked.

"Just the truth," she said, "and the answer to the question: How do you want to be remembered?"

Henderson gaped, then snapped his mouth shut.

"Mr. Henderson," said Val, "let's be honest with each other, shall we? Along with being a multiple murderer, you also have delusions of grandeur—a need to let people know how smart you are. The truth is, your clues were childish. All you had going for you was a head start, and that you buried most of your clues."

"Bullshit!" Henderson's deeper voice returned. "My clues are masterful. Unique. They're elegant in ways you idiots don't understand!"

It is all an act, Val thought. *Good. Let's get the real him out in the open.*

"Want to know how we found the names on Senior Walk? My cousin's son read about the stars, tracked them all down, and figured the rest out in a couple of hours. He's a high school sophomore, Mr. Henderson."

"No, you're lying," Henderson muttered.

Cal nodded to Val as if to say *"It's working."*

Serial killers needed to feed their egos. She, Cal, and Ted would wound Henderson's ego enough to get him talking.

"It was your bad luck that this kid has a relative who works for a federal agency," Val said.

"FBI? NSA?" Henderson asked.

"A federal agency," Val said repeated. "All he had was a list of names. When he called me for help, I couldn't believe it. One of the murders happened right down the road from my field office. How stupid do you have to be to try something like that in Northern Virginia?"

"Stupid?" Henderson said. "It took you seven years and a stroke of dumb luck to find me."

"Whatever you say, Mr. Henderson," Val said. "I went out to the forest where you dumped that girl's body and found the presents you left. Again, a childish puzzle. That led us to Colorado, which led us back to Arkansas. And here we are because you just couldn't stay off Facebook."

Cal and Ted started laughing.

"Fuck you," Henderson snapped. "I want a lawyer. You're detaining me illegally."

"Lawyer?" Val mocked him. "Why? You haven't been arrested."

"Then what the hell are you holding me for?" Henderson snarled.

"Like I said," Val continued, "we want the truth—the rest of it, anyway. You must have hidden more boxes; left more clues. But why go crisscrossing the country playing your game when we can just ask you? That note in the book may as well have been an engraved invitation."

The big man was sweating through his clothes. "Let's say I give you get the rest of the story. What then?"

"There's is no 'What then,' Maliq," Val turned to Cal. "Would you help me up?"

Cal helped her to her feet and handed her a liquid-filled syringe.

Henderson's eyes bulged. "What the fuck is that?"

"You ever heard of Norflex, Mr. Henderson?" Val asked with a coolness she didn't feel. Playing someone so different from herself was nerve-racking but also exhilarating. And the pleasure she was taking in it pained her conscience.

He's a killer, Val reminded herself. *He's the reason six women and three men are dead; the reason my brother lost seven years of his life.*

Cal supported her as she hobbled over to Henderson. "This is a Norflex variant," she said. "It's less detectable and more lethal than normal. At this dosage, most subjects succumb within three hours. But at your size, I give you five."

"Get that shit away from me," Henderson fought to tip the chair over.

Ted stepped in from behind, steadied the chair, and pressed the shotgun to Henderson's ear. "Keep it up, smart guy, and you'll get a buckshot injection to the head instead of what's in that needle."

"I'll talk," the big man blubbered. "My manifesto has everything you need to know."

"Manifesto?" said Val. Their search hadn't turned one up. "Where is it?"

"Hidden," said Henderson. "I was going to mail out copies when I was done. I have notebooks, too."

Val brandished the syringe. "You'll have five hours once I administer this."

Ted covered Henderson's mouth with a hand towel. She slid the needle into the big man's muscular arm and depressed the plunger with a well-practiced motion.

The serial killer's eyes widened even more, and he moaned beneath towel. Soon, he began to weep.

Cal walked Val back her chair. She sat down and waited for him to quiet down before she spoke again. "I asked you before, how you want to be remembered, Mr. Henderson. Now there are only two ways you *can* be remembered: as a proficient serial killer on par with the Zodiac, or as a common pervert ridiculed by everyone who ever knew you."

He shot her a terrified look.

"My associates and I just want to fill in the missing pieces. Your case could earn us promotions. Maybe a book deal or a Netflix show. We don't want the local PD or some fucking DA taking credit when we've done all the heavy lifting. So tell us what we need to know, and you'll get the notoriety you've worked for."

Ted removed the towel. "I told you," Henderson sobbed. "It's all in my notes … my manifesto."

"Where?" Val demanded.

Henderson's lip quivered. "I'm already dead. Why should I help you now?"

"Because if you don't tell us everything, your body will be found hanging in a closet with your undies around your ankles and your dick in your hand. You'll just be another sad casualty of autoerotic asphyxiation."

Henderson lunged. The chair creaked as he strained against his ropes at arm's length from Val's face. Ted grabbed the chair again and held it steady.

Cal stepped between his wife and Henderson. "Don't like that alternative, you sack of shit? Shoulda thought of that before you chopped up those girls. Start talking, motherfucker. Where's your manifesto?"

Henderson's cheek twitched. His tears flowed freely. "In the tornado shelter. In the garage."

Cal straightened up, and Val remembered him mentioning handles on the garage floor.

"There's no alarm or other surprises waiting for us if we open that shelter, right?" Cal grilled Henderson.

"An alarm," Henderson stammered, a shell of the man who'd held her at gunpoint, promising to skin her face off.

What a weird day. "You two take turns searching the tornado shelter and the bedroom," Val told her two masked helpers. "You first, Mertz."

With a nod, Cal headed for the tornado shelter. Ted stood

guard over the killer.

"Now," Val said to Henderson, "What's your real name?"

"Alastor St. John."

"Where are you from, Alastor St. John?"

"Bowie, Tennessee."

"Never heard of it."

A glint appeared in the killer's eye. "No surprise, there. It's just a nothing town. But that's where it all started ... when I'd go to the hillside to watch the road."

Val listened in morbid fascination as the monster told her how he'd come to be. He told her about Peaches and Gay Weed Hankinson. About his mission and the Mousetrap.

And about the other murders.

TWENTY-FIV_

From the *New York Times*, July 17, 2019:

"What's Hiding Within the *Nothing Hides Forever* Podcast?"

An FBI raid on a suburban home rocked an upscale Columbia, Missouri neighborhood last week. Now, news leaked from an allegedly related serial murder case is sending ripples through true crime forums.

A purported manifesto was mailed to several news outlets, including the *Times*. Resembling a diary, the sixty-page document attributed to the resident of the raided home calls for violence against Whites in America. It also contains what appear to be confessions to multiple murders committed over the span of several decades.

The manifesto has sparked a firestorm of controversy, not only for advocating racial violence, but because it appears to exonerate a number of individuals who were prosecuted for the author's confessed crimes. Three men convicted of murders detailed in the manifesto have already received the death penalty. Three others remain on death row.

The *Times* reached out to the FBI regarding the raid, its

connection to the manifesto, and the identity of its author, referred to in the text as "the Fulcrum," but no response was forthcoming as of press time.

Meanwhile, Denis Lay, creator of the wildly popular *Nothing Hides Forever* podcast, has also been tight-lipped about rumored connections between his series' latest season, *Murder in Arlington*, and details found in the manifesto. Indeed, much of Lay's most recent narrative mirrors some of the events detailed in the manifesto, with only certain names and locations changed.

The silence from law enforcement and Lay hasn't stopped true crime fans from voicing their opinions online.

Many speculate that the *Murder in Arlington* protagonists, Harold and Carol Barrow, are real people. Fan theories identify them as everything from FBI leakers to private investigators to concerned private citizens to pseudonyms for Lay.

Whoever they are, the question remains: Why did the Barrows not make their findings public sooner? The *Times* will cover developments in this unfolding mystery as they emerge.

※ ※ ※

"Well that's some bull." Val skimmed the article on her phone as Addie snuggled closer on her lap. "We never sent a copy to the *New York Times*."

Her daughter had been joined to her at the hip since she and Cal had gotten back a week ago. She'd even insisted on getting the ice packs for Val's injured knee.

"Yeah, but the *Times*' readership doesn't know that," Cal said. "And by the time the correction is made, no one will care. Only the headline counts, everything else is just static."

"At least we know the FBI couldn't suppress the manifesto,"

said Val.

"Which surprises me, because they did scrub anything leading back to Professor McMichael. I haven't seen one article that mentions him owning the house or renting it out."

"I hate seeing Denis' name splashed all over the place," said Val. "He must appreciate all the attention his podcast is getting, but I don't think he's one for the limelight."

"Oh, I don't know about that," Cal said. "I spoke with him this morning, and he said he's kind of enjoying the notoriety. But he did mention getting an email from Apple about his podcast being 'temporarily unavailable' due to some unnamed violation of their terms of service."

"They took down his podcast?" Val sat up and winced as pain stabbed from her knee.

"Only for about a day," Cal said. "Denis is a lot more resourceful than you give him credit for. Did you know he was a liability lawyer in his younger days? He reads stuff like that TOS for fun."

"For fun?"

"He says you wouldn't believe what some companies try to hide in the fine print. Anyway, his show is up and running again."

"You think it was an honest mistake?" she asked with a heavy dose of skepticism. "Or did the feds put in a call in to Apple?"

Cal shrugged. "It's amazing *we* haven't gotten a call yet. Or a visit."

"Maybe they're leery after the little gifts we included along with the manifesto copies we mailed those two investigative journalists."

Her husband chuckled.

Val looked down at her sleeping daughter. "Cal, you don't think they'll come after us and try to take our kids, do you?"

"If they could have, they would have already. They can't prove we were in Missouri because we drove, used burner phones, and paid cash for everything. Maybe some surveillance camera caught us with our hats off, but so what?

We gifted the FBI a serial killer, alive and willing to talk."

"I wish I could have been there when he woke up and realized he got tricked," Val said.

"What was it you gave him again—saline solution?"

"Yes, we use it to flush out IV lines. His body absorbed it without a trace it in no time." Val rolled over, placed Addie on the other side of the couch, and moved a lock of sandy hair off the girl's face to watch her sleep.

"Do you think we're in the clear?" Val asked.

"The only person I'm worried about is Ted. He *did* fly to St. Louis, so they can track him that far. He's told me not to worry, so I guess I won't."

Val broached the question she burned and dreaded to ask. "What about Julian?"

"We'll give them till the end of the month. Then we go public, force their hand."

"What if they deny it?"

"I don't think they dare play dumb. But if they try to make us settle for a commuted sentence, we'll see how they like people hearing the rest of the story."

※ ※ ※

From the *Baton Rouge Courier*, July 19, 2019:

"Decades-Old Execution of Man Convicted of Murdering LSU Student Under Scrutiny"

On October 11, 1986, Louisiana State University teaching student Patricia Greere disappeared from the State Fair in Baton Rouge. Her body was found days later in an abandoned warehouse.

Police picked up homeless Vietnam War veteran Reginald King after an anonymous call implicated him in the crime. Evidence found at the warehouse linked King to the murder, and he was later tried and convicted. He was executed in 1990.

Throughout the trial and up to the time of his execution, King maintained his innocence.

A recently surfaced manifesto from a person known only as "the Fulcrum" has shed new light on Ms. Greere's murder and Mr. King's possible false arrest and execution.

The manifesto also raises concerns as to whether "the Fulcrum" was not only known to the Baton Rouge Police Department, but involved with them in some professional capacity.

From the *Arkansas Telegram*, July 19, 2019:

"Podcast, Manifesto Cast Serious Doubts about Springdale Man's 1997 Execution"

Springdale Police Chief Dallas Huckabee held a press conference today, addressing speculation about a decades-old murder.

True crime podcast *Nothing Hides Forever* sparked the controversy in a series of recent episodes suggesting connections between the 1992 slaying of a University of Arkansas student and a manifesto circulating online. The manifesto's author claims responsibility for the murder of psychology student Dawn Stewart and the subsequent framing of Curtis Latimore, a Springdale truck driver put to death for the killing in 1997.

In a further bombshell, the manifesto mentions several former police officers by name, including former Springdale police chief Caleb Huckabee, the current Chief's uncle.

Huckabee declined to confirm or deny any ongoing investigations into these claims. The Chief stated that to his knowledge, the Springdale and Fayetteville police departments pursued every appropriate avenue in the case. He went on to express his confidence in the officers involved and ruled out any official misconduct.

From *The Centennial*, July 20, 2019:

"Death Row Inmate Convicted of Adams State Student Slaying Hopes for Retrial"

From the *Dallas Tribune*, July 22, 2019:

"Family of Iraq War Veteran Executed in 2013 Calls for Justice, Vindication"

From *The Atlanta Herald-Observer*, July 23, 2019:

"New Evidence Leads to Appeal for Man on Death Row for 2015 Murder"

From the *Beltway Tribune*, July 26, 2019:

"Manifesto May Bring Reprieve for Virginia Death Row Inmate"

It's been five years since Julian Gutierrez received a death sentence for the kidnapping and murder of George Mason University student Kayla Reynolds. Now, a controversial manifesto may change the condemned man's fate.

Reynolds went missing from her dormitory in the fall of 2012. A week later, her body was found near the Spotsylvania Civil War Military Park. In the early morning hours of October 25, police responding to an anonymous tip spotted Gutierrez driving by the scene. After pulling him over, sheriff's deputies found damning evidence in his car linking him to Reynolds' abduction and slaying.

Despite that evidence, Gutierrez maintained his innocence throughout his trial. In 2014 he was found guilty on multiple charges including kidnapping and first-degree murder. He was given the death penalty and remains on death row awaiting his October 5 execution.

But an unlikely turn of events may offer Gutierrez a reprieve. Anonymous sources say new evidence contained in a manifesto by a person in FBI custody may cast doubts on the convicted killer's guilt.

These confidential sources suggest that the manifesto's author, self-identified as "the Fulcrum," is the same individual removed from a Missouri residence by FBI and BATF agents earlier this month. Federal investigators have yet to confirm the manifesto's authenticity.

Governor Mike Rathem's office has issued no formal comment on the matter, saying only that Gutierrez's consideration for a sentence commutation or pardon will depend on the relevant federal agencies' findings.

※ ※ ※

Val and Cal paid a visit to the FBI's office in Quantico a few weeks after the manifesto story broke on national news. And they brought an attorney.

Dale Danskitt had reached out to them, saying, "A little bird that draws atrocious caricatures told me you might be in need of legal representation."

Danskitt insisted on working *pro bono*. He owed Carrington, and the media exposure wouldn't hurt his practice, either.

The first agent seated across the big conference table insisted the Coopers didn't need a lawyer since they weren't under arrest.

"You know what 100 percent of police officers, DAs, and

judges say when asked if they'd talk to law enforcement without a lawyer present?" Danskitt asked.

"Suit yourselves," the agent said.

For two hours, various agents asked Val and Cal the same questions twice—once for each of them, with slightly different phrasing. Each time, Danskitt shook his head and said, "I wouldn't answer that."

Val could tell why. The feds weren't subtle about trying to get her and Cal to give up more clues and incriminate themselves in the bargain.

When the soft interrogation was done, most of the agents filed out. One remained, silent and fuming: Mertz.

A few minutes later, an older man projecting an air of authority walked in and sat down. "I'm Assistant Director Schultz. Now, is there a reason you're both so reluctant to answer our questions?"

Danskitt answered. "With all due respect, Assistant Director, what's in it for my clients if they do answer?"

Schultz frowned at the couple. "Failure to cooperate may arouse suspicions that you have something to hide."

"Respectfully," Danskitt said, "that's the pot calling the kettle black. The truth will come out, whether it's revealed by you or someone else. The Bureau has a lot to lose, and has a lot of highly motivated competition. So again, what's in it for my clients?"

"Knowing they provided much-needed closure to families of the victims and the falsely accused," said Schultz. "Not to mention helping Mrs. Cooper's brother."

"Not without immunity," the lawyer said.

"Immunity?" Schultz's brow furled. "From what?"

"Reprisal, for one. Like it or not, *if* the Coopers have information that makes the case against the man you have in custody, the names of several law enforcement agencies nationwide will be mud. Second, *if* the Coopers participated in necessary but technically illegal activity in the pursuit of justice, they would want assurance that any charges would be waived before they talked to you."

"I assure you, Counselor," said Schultz, "that reprisal against the Coopers from any agent of this Bureau would constitute a vanishingly remote possibility."

"Not so remote," Danskitt shot back, "given that Mrs. Cooper was already confronted by one of your agents in a most inhospitable way."

"When was that?" the Assistant Director asked.

"June 29, around 0815," said Val. "A Saturday. I was just getting off my night shift."

"You seem to be sure about that date," the Director responded.

"Whenever my children are threatened, it gets burned into my brain." Val flicked her eyes to Mertz. "Call it a character flaw."

"Threatening your …" the Director looked at Mertz, who lowered his eyes.

Not so tough since we sent those investigative journalists his cards along with copies of St. John's manifesto. "I believe the phrase was 'your children would have to be placed with Child Protective Services in the event of you and your husband's arrest,'" Val said coldly.

"I see," Schultz said.

TWENTY-SIX

From the *Chicago Tribune,* **August 25, 2019:**

"Virginia Couple Who Inspired Viral Podcast Seeks to Free Woman's Brother from Death Row"

We don't have to wonder who Carol and Harold are anymore.

For those who've been hiding under a rock, the true crime podcast *Nothing Hides Forever* has become the latest internet phenomenon. And for reasons as shocking as they are novel.

The show broke the barely fictionalized story of a real serial killer active from the mid-1980s to 2015. A recently released manifesto detailed the man's grisly crimes and the twisted motives behind them. And that's not the most astonishing part.

Alastor St. John (alias Maliq Henderson), framed innocent men for the murders he committed. Three of those men have been executed, and three others are on death row.

But even that's not the half of the story.

Yesterday the FBI announced that Valentina and Calvin

Cooper of Richmond, Virginia are the real-life inspirations for Carol and Harold Barrow, the new protagonists of the latest season of the *Nothing Hides Forever* podcast. Valentina, whose brother was allegedly framed by St. John for a 2012 murder, met series creator Denis Lay at CrimeMeet, a true crime convention held in Chicago earlier this year.

After weeks of silence, Lay confirmed that he and the couple had coordinated the show's narrative during their months-long investigation. Asked how he kept listeners from linking his dramatizations to the real crimes, Lay said, "We had to obfuscate some of the details—changing Colorado to Utah, for example; and inventing a fictional college to stand in for the University of Arkansas. Even that wasn't quite enough, though. A few anons from 4chan related some of the clues to one of the actual murders."

At a press conference attended by Virginia Governor Mike Rathem, Mrs. Cooper gave the following statement:

First and foremost, I want to tell the families of the murdered women — in particular the family of Kayla Reynolds — that our hearts go out to you. Though we were fighting, and continue to fight, for my brother's freedom, we never forgot that an innocent woman's life ended far too soon. I pray that everyone wounded by these crimes can find peace and closure.

I extend heartfelt condolence to the families of Reginald King, Curtis Latimore, and Tyrique Oliver. They did not deserve to be taken from this life, and I can only pray that having their good names restored gives them a measure of peace. I would like to thank the FBI and ATF for helping my husband and me, and our supporters, bring Alastor St. John to justice.

Asked if she knew how the *Mousetrap Manifesto* was leaked to the media, Mrs. Cooper had no comment.

※ ※ ※

"They're calling him the SJW Killer, did you know that?" Val watched her son and daughter playing at the park near their home. Addie would turn seven in three weeks, and Val was already planning a dinosaur-themed birthday party.

I just pray her uncle will be there.

The Governor had already stayed the execution, but he was waiting for the House of Delegates to vote on an appeal.

"Better than the 'SEC Killer' nickname that almost caught on," said Cal.

"College football fans in the South were not happy." Val laughed despite herself.

He loved seeing the warmth return to her face, the stress seeping out. For this reason, Cal hadn't mentioned the support he'd noticed St. John was getting recently. Social media posts and online groups publicly stating that "The Fulcrum" had a valid point that America was a force of evil rooted in racism. Some going so far as to justify his actions.

Is this country irrevocably divided? Have the forces working to get the American public to hate each other won?

But Cal thought about Jameson and Denis, and especially Mose, Dwayne, and Jasmine. There were still decent people ready, willing to help strangers. *I even met a lawyer that was worth a damn.*

They had gotten the immunity that Danskitt had asked for, and he handed over all the evidence they had collected. The box in the forest and in Colorado, the database of names from Senior Walk, and they had had several hours-long conversations with agents about their process and conclusions.

The feds had talked with Ted and the Arkansas Crew as well, though the agents assured them that it was strictly for the completeness of their files. Cal was sure to inform them that no one other than Ted and themselves knew the extent of what any of the evidence meant.

Still, he had called Dwayne and Mose, to ease his mind that the Fed weren't trying any funny business.

"No, no, they were nice and cordial to us, Mr. Cooper,"

Dwayne said, "My uncle did most of the talking, and I got the feeling they were ready to get out of there a lot sooner than they managed to. Anyway, it was pretty cool to have them over. Gave me some street cred, but I'm not supposed to talk about any of it, so I guess it's pretty worthless."

"Not worthless," Cal reminded him, "it will make a great story to tell your kids about how you and Jasmine got together."

He could almost feel the younger man blushing over the phone, but after a moment Dwayne said, "That reminds me, I'm meeting her folks next week. They're coming up from central Arkansas for the first Razorback game."

"That's good, but I need you to do me a favor," Cal responded. "Don't propose to her until after the new year. Val and I have a bet going, and I think you should wait until after the holidays."

"Jeez, you guys already have my whole life figured out, don't you?" Dwayne said, though with a joy in his voice that only one newly in love can have.

He looked at his wife again, and for a moment with the late day sunlight beaming through the trees, he caught a glimpse of the young woman she had been when he first met her. The past few months had aged her, had stressed her to her limits, had almost killed her. He spent more than a few restless hours thinking about the bullet holes he found in the basement's walls. One as she was trying to get out, and another just as he came charging in. Both missed her by inches.

He had to drop his eyes, to hold back the sudden wave of sadness at the thought of not being here in this moment with her.

She looked at him just then, sensing his shift, and hugged him close.

Epilogue

IN TWENTY-FOUR hours, Julian would be a wanted man.

Not for murder—not anymore—but for his thoughts; for an hour of his time.

Julian would have phone privileges after his transfer from death row.

After years of talking only to the guards, his sister, her husband, and himself, millions would hear his story.

And once the appeal trial is over in a few weeks, or months if I'm unlucky ...

He woke up to the cell he had known for almost five years. If it had gone differently, those familiar walls would only have held him for a few more weeks.

Soon I'll be Out There again.

The thought dazzled his mind like sudden daylight shone in the eyes of a man who'd spent his life in a cave.

How am I gonna manage? How can I live in a world of more than one room?

He thought back to that fall evening; about the man he'd been. For a long time, he'd hated that young aimless kid. He hated that he'd been framed with such ease. The man who had taken him called him the Weakling.

Was that name wrong?

No. That naive kid was a weakling.

Was.

Julian stood up and stared into the stainless-steel mirror. He wasn't that weak kid anymore.

Even the warped visage in the prison mirror was that of a man.

He remembered his birthday, when his sister had come; before the postcard had arrived.

He'd held on to resentment and broken her heart.

Now it was time to think about forgiveness.

Not that he forgave Alastor St. John. Julian wasn't sure he ever could. A monster that had destroyed so many other lives didn't deserve forgiveness.

But maybe in time he could forgive those who had put him in that cell—who would have preferred that he'd been forgotten.

Not that he would let anyone forget.

But forgive? Yes, someday.

But if doing his time had given him anything, it was clarity. About what he wanted from life. And what was important in it. He was done resenting.

Julian knew that his sister and her husband had gone through hell for him. Val wouldn't elaborate, but Cal had mentioned that it could have turned out bad.

Like never seeing his sister alive again bad.

Footsteps clacked down the corridor to his cell. "Julian?" a familiar voice asked.

He turned to the guard who eyed him through the small window. "I'm afraid we can't transfer you, son."

A dense knot formed in Julian's stomach. "What?"

"Warden just got off the horn with the big guy. There's not gonna be an appeal trial."

Julian's throat tightened.

His hands balled into useless fists.

The guard smiled. "They went for a straight pardon."

"They …" Julian's body relaxed as gravity let go of him.

For the last time, the guard opened the door.

He helped Julian collect his books and his writings, and walked him straight down the corridor. The free man spared only a glance at the left-hand path that had once been his fate.

✳ ✳ ✳

Clear Skies
They're all mine
Inside this brain alight.
They can't be touched
By the outside
Or by those with darkened sight.
-The (former) Death Row Inmate

Excerpts and Notes

(Confidential - For Official Use Only)

Synopsis:

The Subject is Alastor Patrick St. John, a fifty-four-year-old Caucasian male, born in Bowie, Tennessee on March 12, 1965. His mother Mary St. John (née Winters) was a homemaker. His father Charles Alastor St. John was a construction worker and soldier who enlisted in the U.S. Army in 1972. Charles was killed in action in 1973 during the evacuation of Saigon.

The crimes described below are according to the Subject's confessions and as outlined in his so-called *Mousetrap Manifesto*.

The Subject graduated high school in 1983 and attended college at Louisiana State University in Baton Rouge, earning a B.A. in sociology in 1988.

During his time in Louisiana, the Subject committed two murders. In 1984, he murdered a thirty-one-year-old stranger named Kenneth Allen LeMont. And in 1986, he committed the first of six serial-pattern murders, that of twenty-one-year-old Patricia Greere. Greere was a student at LSU that the Subject had begun following months earlier.

A thirty-seven-year-old homeless man (see: "The Vagrant") named Reginald Donnell King was arrested after police found evidence linking him to Greere's murder. St. John has admitted falsely implicating King via an anonymous call to police. King was tried and convicted in 1987 and executed by the state of Louisiana in 1990.

The Subject began attending the University of Arkansas in 1989, receiving his Master's in Criminology in 1991. The next year, he used his position as a teaching assistant to lure twenty-year-old student Dawn Stewart to a house outside of Fayetteville, Arkansas, where he murdered her.

A thirty-five-year-old truck driver (see: "The Trucker") named Curtis Lamar Latimore was picked up on an anonymous tip mailed to the Springdale Police Department. The Subject stated that he rode along when police apprehended Latimore and led them to evidence he had planted in the suspect's truck the day before.

Latimore was tried and convicted of Stewart's murder in 1993 and executed by the state of Arkansas in 1997.

In 1994 the Subject accepted an assistant professor position in the sociology department at Adams State College in Alamosa, Colorado. In 1998, after having a brief sexual relationship with a nineteen-year-old student named Felicia Budner, the Subject murdered her and hid the dismembered body on the outskirts of Alamosa.

The victim's ex-boyfriend, a nineteen-year-old student athlete (see: "The Runner") named Carlos Ortega, was picked up for interrogation the next day. According to the Subject he suggested that police look into Ortega, citing relationship troubles as a possible motive, after again planting evidence.

Ortega was convicted of Budner's murder in 2000 and was on Colorado's death row until recently. His pardon is described as "imminent" by FBI sources.

Shortly after Ortega's arrest, the Subject acquired a copy of the book *Cauldron of Empires* (see: Cauldron Book). Reading it convinced him that he was a key player in an upcoming race war in the United States.

Transcript: "You have to understand that what I'm talking about is already in motion. The cogs are already turning. I knew I might be caught, sure. I think that part was inevitable. But the Mousetrap is burning down, and all the rot it was hiding is getting revealed. Why do you think I'm talking to you guys right now? For my health? I'm sure you're rolling your eyes, thinking *This is just another Charles Manson, another race war lunatic.* Well, keep thinking that."

In late 1998 the Subject accepted a position at Texas Tech in Lubbock. While there, he sought out a suitable "Vessel" for his upcoming plans under the guise of mentoring at-risk youth. The Subject detailed that he was looking for a young African-American man with a height and build similar to his. Choosing a foster program gave the Subject access to young people with few or no familial attachments.

The Subject began fostering sixteen-year-old Maliq Henderson in 1999. Henderson became his legal ward later that year. In June of 2001, the Subject killed Henderson and staged a fiery automobile accident outside Snyder, Texas. The fire consumed Henderson's body, but it was Alastor St. John who was pronounced dead at the scene.

The Subject, having altered his appearance to appear African-American, was known as Maliq Henderson until his capture in 2019.

As Henderson, the Subject received a sizable payment from St. John's life insurance. He enrolled in a community college in Lubbock and was later admitted to Texas Tech. He received a B.A. in Criminology in 2004, and a Master's in Criminology in 2006.

In 2005 the Subject began stalking twenty-one-year-old Texas Tech student Kelsey Ingraham. He abducted and murdered her in November of that year.

A twenty-four-year-old Iraq War veteran (see: "The Warrior") named Tyrique Oliver was arrested in the car where he'd been living after police received an anonymous tip. Oliver, whom the Subject had befriended while working at a food shelter, was found in possession of a bolt-action rifle. Ballistics matched the rifle to bullet fragments from Kelsey Ingraham's body. The Subject admitted to stealing the rifle after having drugged Oliver and returning it after shooting Ingraham's already dismembered torso. Oliver was found guilty of murder in 2007 and was executed by the state of Texas in 2013.

In 2007, the Subject (as Henderson) accepted an assistant professorship at George Mason University in Fairfax, Virginia.

In 2008, the Subject, now forty-three years old, began experiencing heart murmurs. Though tests returned no serious medical issues, the Subject proceeded with his plan to connect all his murders via clues left on the University of Arkansas' Senior Walk (see: "Senior Walk") ahead of schedule. The Subject devised a custom powder-actuated punch housed in what looked like a cane, which he used to mark the sidewalk. These were among the clues deciphered by A and B (see: "Coopers").

As noted by the interview with A, the Subject also revisited the clues left in Colorado (see: "Colorado Box") to direct the finder to Arkansas. The Subject returned in 2013 and again in 2016 to add his most recent murders to the clues on Senior Walk.

In October 2012, the Subject met with George Mason student Kayla Reynolds outside of class on several occasions. On the last, he drugged her and drove her to his residence. He kept her there for several days before murdering her and dismembering her body. The Subject then transported her corpse to the forest in the Spotsylvania Civil War memorial park.

Twenty-three-year-old warehouse worker (see: "The Weakling") Julian Gutierrez (who is B's brother, and A's brother-in-law) was detained after driving past an active investigation scene. A brief search of Gutierrez's vehicle revealed evidence the Subject had planted, leading to Gutierrez's arrest.

Gutierrez was found guilty of Reynolds' murder in 2014 and was incarcerated on death row at Sussex State Prison. Virginia Governor Michael Rathem first commuted Gutierrez's sentence to life in prison, and later the Virginia House of Delegates issued his pardon.

Transcript: "I know you guys think my obsession with Providence is horseshit. But I can recall a dozen times, maybe more, when I just had an absolute angel on my shoulder. This was the only time I took the guy to the scene. I mean, his prints and everything were all over the place. So as soon as local PD got the dogs out, they would have found where I buried her and had this kid in no time. So I probably could have waited till daylight. But something told me "Call it in right now," as soon as he drove off after waking up from the chloroform. I followed him to his apartment afterward, and wouldn't you know it? Middle of the night, the idiot drove right back to the scene. You tell me that's not Providence."

In 2013 the Subject accepted an associate professor position at the University of Georgia. After stalking engineering student Taylor Buss for several weeks in 2015, the Subject ambushed her while she was hiking alone and murdered her. The Subject stated that the accelerated timeline was due to another health scare, and his feeling that his age was becoming a liability.

Twenty-four-year-old maintenance worker (see: "The Wanderer") Xaviar Narvaez was picked up days later after the Subject reported him to police for disposing of a bloody backpack. Narvaez was found guilty of Buss' murder in 2017 and has been on death row in Georgia ever since. His case is under appeal with a trial set for December of 2019.

In 2016 the Subject accepted a position as associate professor of criminology at the University of Missouri in Columbia. Over the years the Subject had formed numerous professional relationships not only with police, but with several academic advocates for the abolition of the death penalty. One such relationship, with Dr. Edwin McMichael, led to the Subject accepting the position at the University of Missouri, and subsequently how he came to reside at the house belonging to McMichael at 3288 Thornbrook Hollows Road. (Via the [REDACTED] Program, mention of any association between the Subject and McMichael in major publications has been omitted.)

It is now known that he was planning the murder of a twenty-three-year-old graduate student during the 2019 fall semester.

Notes:

1) Along with the manifesto, several notebooks detailing other murders were found. The Subject called most of these "Erasures of Opportunity." From his descriptions, all of his victims were Caucasian, and most were homeless men. If all the murders described are legitimate, the Subject has killed over forty additional people. Coordinated efforts are

underway to identify victims, though many will likely be John/Jane Does.

2) Police and federal authorities have launched an investigation into the death of D.K. Bruenn, a prominent Dallas lawyer found beaten to death outside his fire-gutted office in 2012. Bruenn was building a case to overturn Tyrique Oliver's death sentence on grounds of police misconduct in the collection of evidence. The attempt fell apart after Bruenn's murder and the loss of crucial information in the fire. The Subject dedicated several pages of one notebook to detail how he stalked and murdered Bruenn to prevent him from exonerating Oliver.

3) Forensics experts are working to match a cleaver recovered at the house in Columbia to other killings, possibly requiring the exhumation of victims.

4) Investigations are also underway to find the rest of the self-implicating clues the Subject left in the cases of Greere, Stewart, Ingraham, and Buss.

Transcript: "I really hope you guys make the time to read the book. Especially all you White fellas. It'll be good for you. Nice to know what the future holds for you and your families, you know? Some of you probably think you're safe, that the hand your ancestors played in the strangulation of black lives has been forgotten. But History and Providence have long memories, man, and the time of burning jesters is almost upon us. 2020 will be an interesting year, I think. And I need you to understand that the men who were executed because of me didn't die in vain. They will be remembered as martyrs after the revolution that's to come. Don't think it's lost on me that the only men that got executed were black. With any luck the weight of their deaths will be just enough to bring the plank down on the fulcrum of our final justice. And your final judgement."

Acknowledgements

The author wishes to thank his wife, Rebecca, for the many years of a happy marriage, and her support for his writing endeavors. Also for being the inspiration for the female protagonist in this story.

He would also like to thank his sister, Adelaida, for being his sounding board while he struggled with and overthought plot points, and for reading through the first drafts as he attempted to unearth this story.

He thanks all his Twitter homies, y'all know who you are, for the continued support and encouragement while this book finally got completed.

And a special and heartfelt Thank You! to his editor, Brian Niemeier, for making this book what it is today. Your honest feedback and supreme skill revealed a gem of a story that I didn't know was hiding in this mess I handed you.

About the Author

Abraham spent his formative years in rural Colorado, where he was born. He has also lived in Northern Nevada, Virginia, and Northwest Arkansas. These disparate environments and local cultures have had a great impact on Abraham's view of America and his writing styles. He is the author of the anthology *Going Gone* and various short stories. Visit his website at AbeLopezAuthor.com

Excerpt of Going Gone

THE JEWEL THIEF

In order to allow for new growth, the old must often be felled, burned away to the ashes. This is as true of forests as it is the constructs of men.

And as a single thunderous current can engulf an ancient forest in flame, a solitary strike of violence can erase the oldest of men's foundations.

On this day, such a strike of violence unfolded almost perfectly.

Almost.

It began with a group of vehicles methodically making its way from the outskirts of the capital, through the dust-covered streets, and emerging into the open space of the ancient city square. This motorcade moved in precise unison, seeming like a scarab beetle crossing a desert hardpan.

The lead pair of motorcycles, traveling side-by-side, came to a stop just past the main entrance to the embassy. Following closely behind was an out-of-place black limousine, somewhat dusted over, yet shining brilliantly in the midday sun, which was itself followed by a pair of aging military transport trucks. The head and abdomen of this insectile formation were bristling with weapons; the 'cycles had RPGs mounted across the handlebars for easy access to the driver, and rear-facing second riders, conspicuously armed with AK-47s; the trucks, each carrying a dozen armed men in their canvas-covered beds.

After a moment's pause, the doors to the elongated thorax opened almost simultaneously. Several brutish men, whose demeanor and air could only be those of guardians, emerged into the hot Arabian day. Seconds later a small man of indistinct features was helped out of the rear of the limousine. He then began a slow but purposeful walk up the stairs toward the entrance.

The motorcade had already begun moving away, into the crowded street, when the first flashbang went off to the right of the embassy's entrance. This non-lethal grenade, usually used in close quarters to confuse an opponent and render them momentarily vulnerable, nonetheless produced the desired effect out in the open. The trained guardians were instantly put on the defensive, and surrounded the Prime Minister. They began moving him away from the embassy and toward the street in an attempt to regroup with the motorcade.

The motorcade itself had already made its way halfway down the block when it too reacted to the explosion. The driver of the Minister's limousine stopped and attempted to reverse course, but the sudden onslaught of frightened citizens enveloped the vehicle, rendering it temporarily immobile. The men and women attempting to flee the explosion likewise impeded the men in the back of the truck and the motorcycle drivers.

One of those fleeing men, dressed in a flowing but crudely made thawb, made his way behind an abandoned food cart, and calmly observed the security detail's next move from this hidden vantage point. They could again reverse course and head back toward the embassy. Obviously, this was the riskier course of action as it would take them near the source of the original threat, exposing the Prime Minister to any potential enemies lurking there. They could alternately use multiple alcoves and doorways to get back to the protection of the armored limousine.

As that lone citizen had already predicted, they chose the latter, and seemingly safer alternative.

And so, as they attempted to systematically regroup with the motorcade, the citizen pushed a button on the cellphone he was holding, and a second flashbang went off, fifty feet in front of the security detail, and approximately halfway between them and their destination. The armed men, who had by this time dismounted the truck and were running to meet up with the guards, pivoted immediately and began firing at the source of the latest explosion in an attempt to suppress any immediate attack. The host of bodyguards, meanwhile, moved into the nearest enclosed doorway, armed electrons around the Minister's cowering nucleus.

What they didn't know was that buried in the interior wall of that doorway was an improvised explosive device, and, no doubt, the Prime Minister was closest to its lethal core.

The hidden citizen now pressed another button.

The result was not another bright, yet harmless light show, but rather an immediate thump of destruction and carnage. Any remaining citizens huddled behind vehicles, carts, or doorways now retreated in all directions away from this onslaught.

The hidden assassin did likewise, putting on a face of fright and anguish. As he made his way across the open marketplace, he flung the cellphone high into the air, where it hit the side of a building and went careening into a darkened alleyway.

※※※

"How do you catch a jewel thief?" a mentor of his had once asked him. Before he could attempt a guess, the mentor had answered with a smirk, "You hire a better jewel thief."

That neither of them were jewel thieves was not the point. That at the time they both protected some of the most powerful people in the world was. As was the fact that often the most dangerous threat to those powerful people was not some unknown perpetrator, but instead their former associates. Former pieces of an inner circle that knew how the current pieces operated, understood their tendencies and strategies, and most critically of all, could exploit their weaknesses.

A most dangerous threat, indeed, such as he had become.

He now ran more briskly, and disposed of his feigned, panicked face which was replaced by a stoic, unreadable one. He methodically made his way into the labyrinth of the city's underbelly, eager to get out of the city.

All had gone smoothly, with neither he with his pistol on the ground, nor the sniper on the roof being required. Throwing the cellphone away had been the "all clear" to the sniper and two spotters, who would by now be making their way to their respective exits.

He was just about to make a sharp turn toward his own exit, when he realized he'd picked up a tail. It was nothing more than a momentary overlap of sunlight on cloth, as the man beneath that cloth moved closer to him in the otherwise darkened street, but it was enough to tell him that someone had marked him and was in pursuit.

Damn, he cursed to himself. He was so close to his escape, and had been so sure that in the stampede of people surging away from the explosion he couldn't have possibly been spotted.

Another of his mentor's lessons came to him: Why do we make sure to lock the door once the jewel is stolen? The simplest mistakes are often the most costly. You pick the lock to get in and steal the jewel, but you should make sure to lock the door as you leave, to ensure your crime goes unnoticed for as long as possible.

Had he left a door unlocked?

As he made his first attempt to lose his pursuer, an eerie intuition told him he had.

❈❈❈

"So it can be done?" his contact had asked in their final

meeting, almost four months before. Behind the man's air of calm and arrogance was a tight nervousness to which the assassin had grown accustomed to hearing from clients. His employers (or their middlemen) had such balls at the onset, but they always grew nervous and fidgety as the zero hour loomed closer. This man was better at hiding it than most, but still, the slightest tremble could be detected as he spoke the target's name. "Saiid can be gotten to?"

"Of course," the assassin answered after a moment's pause. "Anyone can be gotten to. Presidents and Popes and Heads of State can all be gotten to. Will you pay my price, though? I'll likely never be able to work again. And disappearing takes money." This was a lie. He'd take some time off, of course, but he didn't want the likes of this fellow knowing he'd be out there on the hunt again.

The arrogant man was already waving a hand in the air, as if the vast sum that he had asked for was of no consequence. "It has already been arranged, my friend. As long as there are no mistakes, your price will be paid."

He began to rise from his seat, when the arrogant man asked, "I do have one more request. Rather, my partners in this endeavor have a request…"